LONGER

ALSO BY MICHAEL BLUMLEIN

LONGER

MICHAEL BLUMLEIN

A TOM DOHERTY ASSOCIATES BOOK

NEW YORK

LONGER

Cover photographs: astronaut © David & Myrtille / Arcangel

Images; sky © Shutterstock.com

Cover design by Christine Foltzer

Edited by Ann VanderMeer

A Tor.com Book
Published by Tom Doherty Associates
175 Fifth Avenue
New York, NY 10010

www.tor.com

Tor® is a registered trademark of
Macmillan Publishing Group, LLC.

ISBN 978-1-250-22980-9 (ebook)
ISBN 978-1-250-22981-6 (trade paperback)

First Edition: May 2019

To Hilary

Although our information is incorrect, we do
not vouch for it.

—**Erik Satie**

Science is properly more scrupulous than
dogma. Dogma gives a charter to mistake, but
the very breath of science is a contest with mistake, and must keep the conscience alive.

—**George Eliot**

The true length of a person's life . . .
is always a matter of dispute.

—**Virginia Woolf**

LONGER

–ONE–

Your vision is not limited by what your eyes can
see, but what your mind can imagine.*

One life was enough. Two were more than enough.

It was time to end it.

Yes.

No.

It would end itself. The last mystery.

Yes.

No. Not the last. But a great one. A great mystery,
unspooled.

Birth was the first, also great.

Rebirth, not so much, and jarring. Overrated.

The stars were bright in the heavens, no atmosphere to
dim them. So many of them, and so many more unseen.

---

*   Colonel Ellison S. Onizuka

So many worlds. So many questions. So many answers.

Yes to all possibilities. Infinity promised this.

But space was cold. Eternity, also.

He'd need a better coat.

He needed one now, because he was shivering.

. . .

He stood in the cupola, gazing at the Milky Way, observing in himself the balance between what he saw and what he felt, between the sensation of cold and his perception of the sensation, and in the latter the balance between awe and terror, which shifted as all things shifted, and which he had experienced his whole life when gazing at the stars and the infinity of space. Currently, terror held the upper hand: how else to explain the chill?

He called on awe to put in an appearance. Humbly, dispassionately, he requested an audience. Sometimes it listened.

Now was one of those times. He knew immediately, because instantly he felt better. Warmer. More hopeful and optimistic.

Gunjita was in the lab mod, pipetting. She hadn't done this in years. Hadn't needed to: postdocs and underlings did it for her. Later, as her once agile fingers became gnarled and crippled with age, she couldn't have done it if she'd wanted to. She could barely hold a spoon. Now her fingers were fine. And there were no underlings. She was alone, but not lonely. Work, as always, was a faithful companion.

Thumbing the plunger was familiar, repetitive, and soothing—press release, press release. It felt good in and of itself, all the better because it freed her to think. She had juved at the age of eighty-two, which, all things being equal, was the current recommendation. Since all things were never equal, some people chose to do it at seventy, or sixty, or even ninety. But statistically speaking, eighty-two was optimal, representing the best balance between benefit and risk.

Broadly, statistics were helpful, but they lacked pin-pointability. A single individual could easily fall outside the range of prediction. Following standard practice, a person might wait too long, or alternatively, juve too soon. Something more precise, impossible to ignore or misinterpret, would be useful.

An idea had been brewing in her mind, and when she was done with the pipette, she went looking for Cav, to run it by him. She found him where she expected she would, staring into space, which had been his main occupation of late, even before news that an extraplanetary probe was on its way. He was a wool-gatherer by nature, and she took a moment to observe him unannounced.

He was a handsome man, and to handsomeness age had added dignity, but it had bent his once fine, long frame, etched his face, slowed his step and also his brain. She wondered how long he was going to wait before juving. The longer he did, the greater the benefit, but also the greater the risk. She observed herself—thoughtful, deliberate, a person who set the bar high and left no stone unturned—pleased that she *hadn't* waited.

"You know that thing mice and rabbits do before they're sacrificed?" she asked.

He didn't answer.

"Cav?"

"Yes?"

"The way they go all calm and limp?"

"Mice? Do we have mice?"

"No. Not here. I'm just thinking about what happens."

"The word, I believe, is resignation."

"They know what's coming. They have a premonition."

"They teach us a valuable lesson. Terror can be tamed. The question: which is better? Which is braver? Resistance or surrender?"

He turned from the window, facing her. "The stars are beautiful tonight. Have you ever seen such beauty?"

"I've been working," she said.

"Also beautiful."

"When others do it."

"I should help."

"I've been remiss."

"Do you need me?"

"I'm fine," she said, having made her point. "I'm enjoying myself."

He smiled, happy to hear it. "I'm a lucky man. I feel rich, Gunjita. Blessed in nearly every way. Does our probe have a name?"

"Eurydice. You don't remember?"

"Who named it?"

"I have no idea."

"I would have named it Orpheus. We should be able to see it soon. I wonder what it's bringing us."

The images the probe had sent back were hazy and of low resolution, showing an indistinct object lighter in color than the asteroid on which it had been found. Efforts to lift or otherwise dislodge it from the asteroid had failed, but in the process the asteroid had cracked, presumably along a fault line or cleavage plane, and a fragment had come loose. As luck would have it, the object, if it truly was an object and not a detection artifact, was on this fragment, which the probe had dutifully snapped up.

"A mineral of some kind, most likely. A discontinuity in the rock."

Cav nodded. "Someone's being careful."

"Yes."

"We should be careful, too. You were talking about premonitions. I'm having one now."

He had his share of health problems, age-related stuff: heart, joints, pisser. As far as she knew, nothing serious, but she didn't know much, because he didn't talk about it much. Wasn't a complainer. She didn't think he was talking about it now.

"Not anything bad, I hope."

"No. Not at all. The opposite."

It was the probe then, as she suspected. "You've got stars in your eyes. The kind of premonition I'm thinking about isn't some dream come true. It's the kind that happens before a catastrophe. Like before a heart attack. Or a stroke. There's a warning signal."

"I'd imagine."

"It's brief. No more than a second or two. After that the damage is done. May or may not be reversible. What if the signal could be stretched out? Instead of seconds, make it last an hour, or a day, or even longer. A month, say. Give people time to do something about it. Take action."

"Juve, for example."

"For example."

"A month of being in a continual state of alarm? Waiting for the ax to fall?"

"Highly motivating, no?"

"Terrifying."

"And it won't fall. That's the beauty."

"Look. There it is."

Far away, a pinpoint of light had separated itself from the infinity of pinpoints around it by virtue of its motion. Slowly but steadily, it scribed its way toward them.

"How will you stretch out the warning signal?" he asked. "What *is* the signal?"

"It's not any one thing. Catastrophe isn't a single event, it's a cascade. There're multiple signals. Most are below our level of awareness. The trick will be to increase our awareness without triggering the cascade. Activate just the right pathways. Block the others."

"Make us more conscious."

"I suppose. In a sense."

"Do you dare?"

"Our bodies sing," she said, quoting him.† "Thousands of songs inaudible to us."

---

† In his vaulting, early years Cav had written a textbook in the form of an epic poem—rhyming no less—an energetic, unruly saga entitled *A Human Ecology*. Reaction was not, suffice to say, uniformly positive, but when is it ever? Gunjita is actually misquoting him slightly. The lines read: Our bodies sing / With music applaudable, / Sweet Lachetic strings / Perfectly pitched, but inaudible.

"For good reason," he said. "We'd be paralyzed if we heard them all. We'd go deaf. Or mad."

He was already hearing too many. Shoulder, back, knees, heart. The songs of age, from the symphony of life.

"The ones we hear are usually the ones we'd rather not," he observed.

"That's the point," she replied.

There wasn't a line on her face. She stood tall and erect, which even in micrograv he was unable to do. She was supple, bright-eyed, energetic. Being with her was like being with a supercharged particle. Simply watching her could be exhausting.

"You're not hearing any, I assume," he said.

"Songs? No. Not a one."

He nodded. Youth was silent that way. In other ways not so much.

"I can imagine what this song of yours will be like," he said.

"Can you? What?"

"Something extremely annoying and impossible to ignore."

"It better be."

"A new line of research for you. A new adventure."

"Not wholly new. But why not?"

• • •

The probe was only the second of its kind. Deep-space mining was in its infancy. Kinks were still being ironed out. So far Eurydice had performed without a hitch. Her lengthy approach was nearly at an end.

Currently, she was in the process of matching her orbit to theirs, close enough that they could see her distinctive dragonfly shape. Her thrusters were pointed away from them, her cone forward. Beneath the cone, held by two robotic arms, like a bee holding pollen, was a large black rock.

Carbon? thought Cav.

All at once there was a glint of light. Then nothing. Then another.

He felt a pounding in his chest. "Is it signaling us?"

"Eurydice?"

"No. The thing on the asteroid."

"It's a reflection, Cav. From the sun. When the probe tilts to the side."

He felt chastened, but not much. "Ice, you think?"

"I don't know. Probably."

She left the viewing port and pulled up the program that controlled the station's external camera array. A few minutes later she had Eurydice on-screen. She repositioned and magnified the image. The asteroid chunk was wide in the middle and tapered at both ends, dolphin-shaped but angular, especially in its lower half, with sharply defined ridges and ledges, likely where it had broken off. Its upper half was more rounded and rippled, as though it had been subjected to weathering of some sort. It looked like a jumbled line of rolling hills. Tucked in the basin between two of them was a lighter-colored shape.

She magnified this.

"Hello," said Cav, who'd been watching.

It looked like a jellyfish with stumpy arms, each of them a different shape and size, irregularly spaced around its circumference. It was dull yellow in color with a hint of green, like week-old celery. It was roughly two hands across, about a finger's thickness. Its surface appeared smooth, fixed, and hard.

"Ameboid," said Cav.

"It's not an ameba."

"I'm not saying it is. I'm saying the appearance. The shape."

"Maybe it was liquid once. Molten. Hardened into that."

"Lava?"

"Why not?"

He knew a bit of geology. Just enough to be dangerous.

"Metamorphic?"

"Possibly."

"Starfish attach to rocks like that," he said, thinking aloud.

Something clinging to something, that's what had popped into his head. Obviously, they weren't looking at a starfish.

"Is it attached?" she asked.

"It wouldn't come off."

"Precisely. It's wedded to the rock. Part and parcel. It *is* a rock."

"But so different." He searched for an explanation. "Could there have been a collision? Say the asteroid was hit by something. This is the impact point. The force of the collision, the heat of it, created what we're seeing."

Her knowledge of geology was about on a par with his. Her knowledge of astronomy, somewhat more advanced. Their expertise lay elsewhere, broadly speaking in the field of human biology, the field of living things. Since living things depended on nonliving things to exist, and since nonliving things obeyed the laws and conditions of physics, it helped to have a broad education, a wide base of knowledge, and an inquisitive spirit.

"Collisions hardly ever happen. And when they do, they're catastrophic. The asteroid would have been annihilated."

"A small collision. With a tiny particle."

"Tiny is right."

"Yes?"

"An impact metamorphosis?" She turned the idea over

in her mind. In biology the concept certainly applied. Sperm and egg the obvious example, and thousands more. "Is there such a thing?"

"Why shouldn't there be?"

This was Cav in a nutshell. Firing salvos, broadsides against dogma and gospel, reality be damned. Flaunting his ignorance, wearing it like a medal of honor. Impertinent. Irreverent. What she loved about him, and what at other times infuriated her. He called it thinking big.

"It's a big universe," he said, right on cue.

They studied it further.

"You know what it looks like?" she said.

"What's that?"

"Puke."

It did have a sheen. And a lumpiness. And a kind of ordered chaos, like a glob, or splat, of something.

"You're right," he said. "That's exactly how it looks. Wonder how it smells. *If* it smells."

"Everything smells," she reminded him, quoting herself.‡

---

‡ From *Smells, Bells,* a far-reaching survey of scent, sensitivity, syntactical stressors, societal sensitization, subliminal sequestration, and so forth. A startlingly significant, statistically sound study, based on her groundbreaking research. Single-handedly, she raised the science of olfaction from the dark ages of genetics and epigenetics into the enlightened era

"To us," he clarified.

"Like puke, I'm afraid." Referencing the power of language, which was the power of suggestion, in this case by a single four-letter word. A mortal blow, or at least a complication, to someone priding herself on objectivity. This was always the risk of thinking. Worse with speaking the thought aloud.

"I've contaminated myself. Have I contaminated you, too?"

"Not a bit." He felt the opposite, as though a gate, or a door, had been opened. "Puke implies a mouth. A mouth implies a living thing."

"I was free-associating," she said quickly.

"Yes. Good. We should."

"It's not living, Cav. How could it be living?"

"Exactly. That's the question. How?"

She could see what was coming. The man just loved getting his head in the clouds, the higher the better. Up where the air was thin, and reality was a long way off. Where you could spin whatever story you liked.

It was a luxury to think like that. Not one she'd had, or

---

of perigenetics (a word first coined by Blumlein more than a century earlier in his classic study of nested personalities and genomics, *Success*). A complete reimagining of the nosology of the nose and the nasal apparatus could scarcely do less.

allowed herself, growing up. She was a practical, orderly thinker, already highly regarded and successful when she and Cav met. He had shown her it was possible to think differently without being: one, completely boring; two, completely self-absorbed; and three, completely useless. He was perceptive. He saw things other people didn't. He wasn't always right, but he was always, or almost always, interesting.

Besides, this thing, whatever it was, was out of the ordinary. Soon they'd have it on board and know much more. For now she'd lose nothing by letting him speculate. She'd even join the party, within limits.

"Rivers have mouths," she said.

"Different kind of mouth. Not what I was thinking."

"Canyons do, too. And glaciers."

He gave her a look. "Do they puke? If so, I'm not aware of it."

"Volcanoes do." Steering him steadily toward reason. In this case, back to lava.

He didn't reply.

He was staring at the image. Captivated.

They'd been married fifty years. She'd always been a patient person. She didn't mind waiting. Good things often came to those who did.

Only now she felt a little differently. *She* was different. She only had this one last life. Just one. Sixty-plus years.

"Knock knock," she said. "Outer space to outer space.

The entity known as G is waiting."

Still nothing.

She grew impatient. Slowly, Cav changed before her eyes from the man she knew and loved into someone standing in her way. She wanted to grab him, shake him, slap some sense into his head. It would do him good. Do both of them a favor.

"Time's up," she announced.

He nodded absentmindedly.

"I'm getting a feeling here," she said.

"From it?"

"From you. You *do* think it's living."

"Is, or was."

An astounding assertion.

She grabbed him by the neck, and shook.

"Hey!" he squawked.

"Want more?"

"I take it you disagree."

She shook him again.

"Control yourself," he squealed.

"Talk sense. And answer when I ask you a question."

He peeled her hands off. "That's fair. I have one for you. What's going on? You don't seem yourself. Have I done something wrong? Offensive?"

Reasonable questions. The answers were yes and yes.

She was in the grip of something, no doubt about

it. She felt like a runaway train. Dashaud Mikelson, of all people, came to mind. She hadn't thought of him in years. Hadn't wanted to.

"You're hormonal," said Cav. "Is that it?"

He was probably right. It was a common aftereffect of juving. All the major hormones raged. A temporary condition, though on occasion the first manifestation of a lasting personality change.

As a rule, post-juving changes were slight: a little more this, a little less that. Gender, in particular, was prone to shift and recalibrate, as all things essentially fluid to begin with did. Usually the shift was subtle, and always enlightening.

But a slap upside the head?

"Consider it a hypothesis," said Cav, extending the olive branch.

She wasn't in the mood for olives quite yet. "I'm sorry, but no. Living doesn't deserve the rank of hypothesis. Something else maybe. Lower in the pecking order. Let's see. Help me out here."

He knew what she was driving at. "Wishful thinking?"

She snapped her fingers. "Bingo."

"It's more than that."

"We've been through this before," she reminded him.

By "we" she meant Earth. By "this" she meant, of course, the Hoax.

"Life does exist elsewhere," he said.

"I don't disagree."

"We won't necessarily know it when we see it."

This was the canon. One of two party lines, the less terracentric, more inclusive. Impossible to disprove.

"It's your dream," she said.

"Yes. Everyone's."

She glanced at the object on-screen. "You're going to be disappointed. I promise you."

"It's possible. Who can say?"

She gave him a look, then heaved a sigh. "You have a feeling about this."

"I do. A hope, for sure."

"I want to honor it. I have a feeling, too."

"You think I'm crazy. I'm losing my marbles."

"I'm frustrated, Cav. I don't understand. Tell me again why you're putting off juving? Because it seems to me that you're intentionally rolling the dice."

"I'm thinking about other things."

"Such as?"

"Do we have to talk about this now?" He couldn't keep his eyes off the screen. "I know it's probably not alive, but what if it is? What *kind* of life could it be?"

"If you drop dead tomorrow, you'll never know, will you? Someone else will find out. Someone else will have his dream come true."

"I'm not dropping dead tomorrow. Why the sudden worry?"

"I'm not worried. I'm curious. What's the point of waiting?"

"I'm not waiting."

"You're not taking action."

He shrugged.

"Because I'm very fond of you. And I know you're fond of me."

"I am. Excessively."

She arched an eyebrow. A slip of the tongue? Or a bad connection? Both were happening more frequently of late. It bothered her not knowing which was which, though not nearly as much as watching him deteriorate. He wasn't just ignoring common practice, he was putting their marriage at risk. She felt unwanted, invisible.

"Exceedingly, I believe, is what you meant."

"Exceedingly what?"

She stared at him. Kindness and concern bent beneath the weight of anger and self-preservation. "Maybe one life together is enough."

He froze, like a deer in headlights. "What do you mean? What are you saying?"

"I'm asking. Do you want out?"

"No. I don't want out. How can you ask? I love you. Exceedingly."

She wasn't amused. "Then why are you distancing yourself?"

He had no reply to this. It was true. He had been. Not intentionally, or mostly not. It was a natural part of growing old. The pulling in of feelers, the gradual encapsulation, the cutting of ties, in preparation for the final, the ultimate separation.

Withdrawal, then adios.

Fortunately, there was an antidote to this.

Juvenation had changed the face of life on Earth. He'd done it once, no questions asked. Life was simply too precious not to.

This time, for some reason, he was dragging his feet. A counterweight, counterargument, had been steadily asserting itself.

Opposed to it, all the things he would leave behind and miss. Gunjita chief among them, never less than a potent, eloquent argument to live, and now in the bloom of youth.

"You're right," he confessed. "I have been. I'm sorry."

"Is something wrong? Are you sick?"

"I'm fine."

"Because this thing, whatever it is, is a golden opportunity, Cav. It's a gift. From outer space. C'mon. The great unknown. Don't you want to study it?"

"Of course. I plan to."

"Thoroughly. Piece by piece. Molecule by molecule. Atom by atom, if necessary. Every way possible."

"It could take weeks. Months."

"Years," she said. "We get three lives, Cav. It's not that many."

His first two had been rich beyond all expectation. What could a third reasonably add? How much wealth did a man need, could a man absorb?

The answer: How could one mind be so hungry for knowledge and experience? And one woman so incredibly beautiful?

"I want to eat you," he said.

"Me?"

"I love you."

"Excessively. I know." She fiddled with the screen. "We need better resolution."

"What we need is a closer look."

"Ninety-six minutes," she said.

–TWO–

Green is the valley
Blue is the night
Out of the shadows
Into the light . . . *

Gleem One, their present home, took its name from Gleem Galactic, the company that spawned it. The station was one of eleven in orbit, all but two private, and the only one of the lot not dedicated to ozone remediation, energy development, climate abatement, extreme sports, or defense. Gleem Galactic took its name from Laura Gleem, a rags-to-riches story—spanning three lifetimes—they wrote books and made movies about, also plays, including a musical, panned by critics, adored by fans, and hugely successful. From drug pusher to drug

---

* From "The Valley," by Los Lobos.

rep, then saleswoman-of-the-year, of what was at the time the world's second largest pharmaceutical company. Then sales director, overseeing a half-trillion-dollar operation. Five years later, after juving for the second and final time, she became CEO.

Her first act as chief was to deep-six the old corporate name in favor of her own. Her second: invest heavily, some said recklessly, in outer space. In particular, low- to mid-orbiting space stations. Future homes for drug production was her thinking, skirting the laws and limits of production on Earth. Not to mention R & D: she foresaw the rise of low and null-grav meds. Had a lab in place years before her competition.

Gleem One just to let everybody know that there were other Gleems on the way. Gleem Galactic because that's where her mind went when her body hurt: somewhere other than Earth.

An unexpected dividend of the station: with a little rearranging, it could double as a treatment center. Gunjita, who kept abreast of such things, had seen this immediately, and at the face-to-face with Gleem's R & D director, Laura, on remote, she and Cav had worked it into their pitch.

So now Gleem was looking at on-site delivery. Already it had its fingers in all other things pharmaceutical, from health to husbandry, agriculture to athletics, procreation to recreation, sewage to cosmetics, so why not? Planetary consumption of drugs, fueled by equal parts need, desire, addiction, the simple habit of everyday life, had never been higher. Gravity-sensitive drugs—small molecules primarily, but also novel pro-and eukaryotic biologics—were the latest craze. The field was just getting started. None of the candidate drugs had been tested in extremely high gravitational conditions—the edge of a black hole, for example, or even Jupiter—and only a few had been tested in extremely low ones, such as outer space. Gleem Galactic was out to rectify this.

Cav and Gunjita were under contract to test H82W8, a tweaked version of one of the linchpin agents used in juvenation, in the hopes of breaking through the so-far unbreakable ceiling of two treatments for any one person. Two treatments, three lifetimes. That was the limit. Two was what you got. Two was safe. More than two, bad things happened. The reports were there for anyone to read. The pictures, if you had the stomach.

Most people didn't.

Finding a way for three to work, and beyond that, for four, five, six . . . for any number of treatments . . . a limitless number . . . was the holy grail of life extension.

H82W8 showed promise, but was unsafe, at least on Earth. How unsafe? Uniformly lethal. Deadly 100 percent of the time. Lethal and deadly were frowned upon in the course of routine treatment, and accordingly, the agent had been re-engineered with a nano-accelerometer insert, a so-called gravitational sensor, which, when activated, led to a change in spatial conformation. Same agent, new shape. New shape, new agent, function following form, as it always did. The questions: one, would the drug remain effective? And two, would it now be safe, at least safe enough?

For the study they had a sample of human cells from a sample of humans, in lieu of an actual living, breathing human person. Surrogate markers weren't perfect, but they were useful. Cells were easy to come by, and relatively easy to manage. They were cheaper by far than whole people. They gave up their secrets much quicker. They didn't complain, at least not audibly. And you didn't get attached to them in quite the same way as you did to a fully formed, fully realized living creature, be it human, monkey, kitty, bunny, or cute little mouse.

Cav had long been a proponent of gravitational testing of biologics. If direct contact were ever to happen with alien life, it would be life that could travel through space. One could imagine a form of life, not to mention of travel, that used gravity not only to navigate and orient itself, but for energy—a kind of food, or nourishment, which was a sine qua non of life. The more you knew about the sine qua nons of life—nourishment, balance, growth, renewal, decay—the greater your chance of recognizing it when otherwise you might not.

Before Gleem, he'd been unable to secure funding for this, despite a lifetime of success and a distinguished career, including a host of honors, prizes, and recognitions. Before Gleem came along, there was no money in micrograv bio, and the days of market-blind, not-for-profit (save intellectual profit), and knowledge-for-knowledge's-sake research were all but extinct. They'd vanished along with the dodo of public financing, not to mention unencumbered public financing, which was truly a dinosaur. Virtually nothing existed in the field of astrobiology, which had dried up more or less completely after the Hoax.

Gleem was an oasis. Sanity in a storm.

It hadn't hurt that Gunjita had agreed to partner with him. She was a major star in her own right. Professor, researcher, pioneer thinker, co-discoverer of CrB, the so-called altruism suppressor gene†, olfactologist extraordinaire. A veteran of the science wars and

---

† Actually, a constellation of genes involved in the regulation of neural and neuroendocrine systems, principally the oxytocin system, that contribute to altruistic behavior. CrB in honor of Hamilton's groundbreaking formula: $C < r \times B$, describing the evolutionary advantage of social behavior, where C represents the costs to the acting individual, B the benefits to the recipient, and r the relatedness between actor and recipient.

of the lab, even more than Cav, who'd come to research relatively late, having spent a good part of his early career as a practicing surgeon.

They had the station to themselves, an anomaly. A series of minor and major crises—a sudden illness, an unexpected pregnancy, a family emergency—had decimated the ranks of the standard five.

Gunjita found the absence of people refreshing, if odd. Labs were like families, and for many years hers had been like large, extended ones. She was used to carving out pockets of silence in the hubbub, where she could think. She did some of her best work in the privacy of her own mind. Solitude nourished her. The only possible thing that rivaled it was collaboration.

She'd been looking forward to collaborating with Cav—it wasn't often their work coincided—but Cav seemed to have other things on his mind. Not entirely. Maybe fairer to say, his idea of collaboration was different than hers. Involved less talk—certainly less directed talk—and longer silences. This had started as soon as they'd stepped foot on the station. He'd turned quiet and even more reflective than normal. As though their research, the very reason they were there, were just a feint, a ploy.

Now Eurydice, with its strange passenger, was docked to the station, and the old Cav was back. Bubbly. Effusive.

A twinkle in his eye. Say what you would, you had to love a man with a twinkle.

Laura Gleem, they said, shot fire from her eyes.

Laura Gleem, they said, was a force of nature.

Gunjita and Cav were indebted to her.

. . .

On the second anniversary of Gleem One's launch, Laura had hosted a get-together on the station. Five handpicked invitees of diverse talents and gifts culled from a watch list of radicals, dreamers, and ne'er-do-wells generated by the DHS, purchased and tweaked by Laura's people to exclude misanthropes, naysayers, finger-pointers, windbags, and bullies. Laura had a fondness for the number five, the color pink, and the letter *k*. The group included a kinesiologist, a knight-of-industry, a remnant Kallikak with something to prove, a kosher Kurdish khan turned propulsion engineer, and Kleptomania, stage name of Ruby Kincade, performance artist and roboticist, who proudly traced her lineage to the Kanuri of central Africa, a striking, outspoken woman and onetime friend of Gunjita, until their terrible falling out. Laura's idea, simplicity itself: put 'em all together with nowhere to go for a brainstorming session. No idea too big or small, too long-or short-termed, too crazy, too pricey. No telling what would happen next. What, if anything, would take root. She had a hunch that something would, was okay if nothing obvious did. Seeds could lie dormant for years. The outcome was unpredictable. That's what appealed to her. That, and being weightless.

Out of that keen, kilowattified, akyphotic klatch, keyed in and karmically attuned, kicking it, no, *killing* it, for three nights and days consec, Eurydice was born. Kraken better fit the tenor of the moment but seemed excessive.

So now, in addition to drugs, Gleem was in the mining business. Which meant the trucking business. Also, navigation. And, of course, exploration. Growing corporate interests of theirs, though still dwarfed by pharmaceuticals.

Eurydice was named in honor of Laura, who, in defiance of expert opinion and every authority on Earth—legal, medical, ethical, theologic—had taken her life in her hands, stared death in the face, and juved for a third time. Ballsy? Try suicidal. No one did it more than twice. She had not been seen in public since.

$\bullet \bullet \bullet$

The probe had already lived up to its name once. Its systems, after crashing somewhere between the outer and inner main belt, had suddenly sprung back to life.

These same systems had guided it flawlessly back to Gleem One, where it now slept. Its two anterior arms, jointed like the insect it resembled, clutched its treasure to what would have been its chest. The object of interest faced outward. The asteroid itself was not huge, but it was bulky. Cav and Gunjita's plan: get some cord around it and reel it into the cargo bay. A tight fit, requiring a guiding hand, but doable. Once in the bay, go from there.

Cav was in the process of suiting up. Got both legs in, then an arm. Needed help with the other, arthritis having done a job on the shoulder. Also needed help with his boots. A couple of months earlier, he was helping her, or rather, two old geezers, they were helping each other.

Gunjita fetched his boots for him without thinking twice. Loosened the buckles, spread the mouths, took one in hand, bent down, about to slip it on his foot, when she was struck by a thought. An image actually, and suddenly her heart was in her throat. The thought came second: her elderly husband was a pair of boots and a helmet away from traipsing out into space.

"No way," she said.

"What do you mean?"

"You're not doing this."

"Don't be ridiculous."

"I'll do it."

"Give me my boots."

"Like I said . . ."

"My boots."

She wouldn't.

"Look at me," she commanded.

She still had trouble believing it herself. Who she was. What she saw when she looked in the mirror. How she felt. Pain-free, comfortable, smooth as liquid when she moved, or rather glided, able to do anything without the slightest effort. She'd forgotten how good it felt.

"Now look at yourself."

He didn't have to. He knew what he'd see. His old, barnacled, parchment skin. His twisted back. His trembling hands. And inside, invisible to the naked eye, the ice pick that was permanently lodged in his shoulder. His weak bladder, his failing heart. So what was new? The march of time never quit.

"You've never done something like this," he said.

"How hard can it be?"

"Like that. Just like that. By underestimating what you're dealing with."

She tapped her head, then saluted. "Judgment good. Brain intact."

"It's dangerous."

"What isn't?"

"You could float off into space."

"I'll be tethered."

He imagined it happening to him, floating away, drifting free, a few hours of oxygen and warmth, then death. Kindly remembered. Quickly irrelevant. Soon forgotten. Separation complete.

Or not. Maybe not. Maybe there was no such thing as separation. Maybe there was cosmic unity, and he'd be one with the universe.

Which would it be?

It seemed worth finding out.

"Okay," he said. "I'll monitor you."

"I'll be careful."

"Fact is, I hate these suits. Too hard getting in and out."

"Your own damn fault."

He held her helmet while she suited up.

"I know you'd love to be the one doing this," she said.

"Next time. How do you feel? Ready to take on the universe?"

"Pretty much."

He didn't want to let her go. He feared for her safety. Pressed the helmet to his chest possessively, protectively, as though it were her.

"Cav?"

"Please be careful." Reluctantly, he handed it to her.

Instead of taking it, she leaned forward and kissed him

on the lips.

He tasted fruity and a little sour. A little tangy. A pleasantly familiar taste, save for the hint of dryness and decay, like the decomposing leaves of an old book.

Hoping to banish this, she kissed him harder, lacing her fingers around his neck, pulling him toward her. A primitive impulse, inarguable and good. Pure chemistry.

The force lifted him, and together they became airborne. Pure physics. They were halted by the module's wall. Cav, who'd been taken by surprise, was jarred into action.

He took her in his arms, or tried to. Their bulky suits made it impossible. It was like hugging dough. They began to somersault, until they hit the opposite wall.

Cav was no gymnast. The tumbling made him dizzy and nauseous. Gunjita was in hysterics. She couldn't keep from laughing. The chemistry, so strong a minute before, was gone.

"Sorry, old man," she said, goosing him tenderly, then donning her helmet.

Cav, meanwhile, had started to get hard. His disappointment was sharp, but fleeting. Age had made him philosophic. Sex required staying powers he didn't always—even often—possess. Sometimes his mind wandered, and he forgot what he was doing. Sometimes his eye fell, not on his beloved Gunjita, where it belonged, but between his own legs, and he was filled with nostalgia. At other times he was grateful. Things could be better, but they could be so much worse. He could still get it up on occasion. If the fates were kind (the drugs no longer helped), it would stay up. From time to time he still thundered like a stallion when he pissed.

"There's no hurry," he said. "You have plenty of time. One foot in front of the other. Nothing sudden. I'll be watching. We'll be in constant communication."

She nodded, and mentally rehearsed their plan. It was straightforward enough. Basically, wrap a cord around the asteroid and bring it aboard. Like roping a horse, which was on her résumé.

She'd ridden and lassoed ponies with Ruby in Iceland, Ruby's adopted home, and where she gave birth to Dashaud. Gunjita had been present at the birth, and as often as she could throughout his childhood. She'd pushed him on the swing, carried him in her arms, fed him, put him to bed. For his fifth birthday she'd bought him a pair of leather boots, to wear while riding the horse that Ruby and Bjorn, his father, had surprised him with. She could still remember the look on his face as they trotted it out. Stunned, disbelieving, reverent. A dream he'd not dared to dream, standing there in the flesh.

She was sixty at the time, and had allowed herself to be coaxed atop a horse of her own.

Through the eyes of babes: it was love at first sight. For

the next two weeks she rode every day. Ruby rode with her. Icelandic horses were prized for their sturdiness and longevity, and she learned to prize other qualities: their temperament, their beauty, and their exhilarating, extra gait.

She'd learned a few basic knots during that and subsequent visits. Hadn't used them in ages, not since Ruby had slammed the door in her face and shut her out. Hadn't ridden a horse since then. Fifty long years. Too painful a reminder.

She could tie a bowline, square, clove-hitch, jerk, figure of eight. Almost any of them would do. The asteroid wasn't going anywhere. It was massive, but weightless.

She got it hog-tied easily enough. What she hadn't counted on was Eurydice itself, which refused to relinquish its prize. Held onto it with a tenacious, possessive, no-you-don't grip. From the beginning Cav had argued strongly and persuasively against trying to forcibly detach the object of interest from the asteroid, which could: one, damage it; and two, damage it irreparably.

Gunjita suggested decommissioning the arms.

"How?" he asked.

"Demolition?"

"Frowned upon by Gleem, I'm guessing. Plus, risky."

"We could cut them off."

Also risky. And difficult. "Any other ideas?"

She was floating beside the asteroid, the nose of Eurydice above her, cone in socket, firmly docked. "I can try loosening the bolts."

He was surprised she hadn't mentioned this first. "Are there bolts?"

She showed him on camera. He located them on a schematic of the probe. Thought it might work.

She got busy. It wasn't long before the asteroid was freed and in motion, she alongside it, guiding it through the cargo doors into the cargo bay, where she secured it, careful to steer well clear of the thing on its surface, which at close range looked slightly larger than they first thought, also slightly thicker, with a hard, shiny surface that concealed what appeared to be a lumpy interior. She reported all this to Cav, whom she eventually joined at the window overlooking the bay.

His nose was pressed against the glass. First contact? Could this be it? He was jelly inside.

Forced himself to calm down and think logically.

He assumed that it was, or had been, living. An improbable assumption, but open to scientific verification. His null hypothesis: it was no different, essentially, from other living things.

Beside him, Gunjita was lost in her own thoughts. Her first impression hadn't changed. The thing was not alive. Not now, or ever. Her null, quite simply, was the opposite.

–THREE–

Nature first, then theory. Or, better, Nature and theory closely intertwined while you throw all your intellectual capital at the subject. Love the organisms for themselves first, then strain for general explanations, and, with good fortune, discoveries will follow.*

They watched it for two days, keeping their distance, observing through the window. This was Cav's way of doing things. Watch. Listen. Smell. Use your senses. Interfere as little as possible. Let nature take its course. Wait.

To watch, they had eyes, and cameras. To listen, ears and mics. Eventually, they'd touch it. What they couldn't do was smell. Too dangerous to smell it directly, and the odorometer only told them so much. Not having smell

---

* From *Naturalist,* by E. O. Wilson.

left a hole in the experience. A question mark. Gunjita liked to say it was tantamount to walking on one leg.

She'd said this very thing the first time Cav had laid eyes on her, in a lecture hall. She was a rising star, and he'd come to check her out. He assumed she was being dramatic, though she didn't seem the type. The longer he listened, the more convinced he became she not only meant what she said, but knew exactly what she was talking about.

Smell began when life began. At the very earliest stages. Smell was basic, primitive, the bedrock of communication. Smell was truthful. Smell was blind. Smell made you fall in love. Smell made you take to the hills. Smell was a rocket, a red flag, an invitation, an alarm.

Cav learned all this and more at that first lecture. He remembered nearly every word, spellbound by the lesson and the teacher. Impossible to say which bound him first, and whether in fact there was a first, his recollection more of a growing, interdependent, virtually simultaneous seduction by speaker and speech.

She'd opened his mind, or rather, closer to say, his mind was blown, which made him all the more aware, now, of what, without the sense of smell, he was missing.

Two days they watched and listened. Cav rarely left the window. He was a scientist, which translated into a Peeping Tom. Living things were meant to be observed.

They were meant to attract attention. Not always, but sooner or later. Being noticed at the wrong time was potentially a death sentence. But at the right time: voilà! Connection. Mutual interest. If the stars lined up, a compatible, coordinated, and, who knew, concupiscent future.

He tried not to think too far ahead. Tried not to get his hopes up. He'd once zoned out on a python coiled on a branch of a Mocambo tree. A magnificent creature, and a rare sighting. He was on a medical mission at the time, doing minor and not so minor surgery in what was left of the Amazon. A day later, after a morning of botfly extractions, he discovered to his chagrin that the snake was dead. A few hours after that he was shocked to find out that it wasn't dead at all, but fake. A practical joke.

He had learned not to pass judgment prematurely.

Gunjita was a member of the same congregation. It rarely helped to jump to a conclusion in science or life, but especially in science. Spontaneity had its place, and occasionally yielded gold, but mostly it didn't. Ninety percent of progress came from slow, methodical work. This suited her, as by nature she was patient and thorough. But after two days she was ready to start running some tests.

Cav resisted: even passive tests ran the risk of altering it.

"How long do you plan on waiting?" she asked.

He didn't have an answer.

"There's work to do," she reminded him. "We're here on business."

"This is more important."

"We have a contract to fulfill."

He grunted.

"You may not care, but I do. You may be done with work. Retired." He hated the word. She was prodding him, fishing. "I'm not. I'm looking forward to many more productive years. I'll need funding. Gleem is a cash cow. It seems counterproductive to spit in their face."

"I see your point," he replied carelessly. His eyes were fixed on the Ooi, the object of interest.

"I'll give you one more day," she said.

He nodded his agreement.

She headed to the lab, where she could be herself without resistance. H82W8 had been acting strangely, flipping out of what should have been a stable shape, as though energized, then flipping back, as though not energized enough. Wanting to change but unable to quite do so. If she could discover the cause, she could eliminate it, and re-stabilize the compound. Then again, if she could discover the cause, she could possibly boost its energy, allowing the grav-sensitive drug to break free of its internal restraints and reassemble itself in a new conformation, maybe closer to what they were looking for, maybe far afield, maybe a dead end, but maybe not. A lab was a kitchen, and Gunjita was a master cook. In the days of the Hoax, when she had her own lab, and defense-related funding was off the charts, she followed her nose to her heart's content, mixing, blending, altering recipes as she saw fit. Now she worked for someone else. And she was on the clock.

She made a note of what she was seeing, intending to investigate it further if she had time. If not, someone else could run with it. She was willing to be the shoulders. Not too terribly invested in this particular study. Science was incremental, and she was incrementally content.

She shot an update to Gleem, then spent some time thinking about biological alarms. Decided to focus on arterial plaque, the cause of most heart attacks, strokes, and related catastrophic events. Plaque was a complex mix of proteins, calcium, and lipids. Scents, on the whole, were much simpler. Could she engineer one to bind to plaque—putrescine, say, or putrescine-like—and as the plaque increased, the scent also increased, to a certain critical level, at which point it got released into the bloodstream, creating a new body odor, as distinctive as the fruitiness of ketosis, say, or the fishiness of uremia, but extra stinky?

She saw no reason why she couldn't. But who would

agree to take it? That was the question.

The answer: anyone who didn't want to die suddenly and prematurely. Cav? Moot point. The lifesaving alarm she envisioned didn't exist.

She had no particular premonition that he *was* going to keel over suddenly and drop dead. His health was slowly declining, sure. She knew how this felt from first-hand experience. But it wasn't as if he was on his last legs. Eighty-four wasn't a hundred and four. Then again, it wasn't twenty-four, or even sixty. Anything could happen at any time, until he juved.

And if something did? She'd lived a whole life without him, so knew that she could. She'd also lived a whole life with, and wasn't finished. Being with him the last two days reminded her of him as a young man, what a mind he had, how far he was willing to go, what a bulldog he could be, delighted with the world, obsessed, provocative, impossible to be with at times, impossible not to be with. She felt that way about him now.

How would she get him to take her lifesaving alarm, if it did exist? She'd offer it, and he'd refuse. In his sleep then? Without his permission? She might as well strap him down and force him to be young.

She'd never do that. She didn't believe in that kind of coercion. Though the idea of straps and physical restraint—of a physical solution to the problem—got her thinking.

She heard a series of beeps. Moments later, Laura Gleem was on-screen, the CGI version of her, which hadn't changed in years.

"Dr. Gharia."

"Director."

Laura's face went through a series of transformations, commentaries and inside jokes on the power of money, imagination, and plasticity, in the process authenticating her identity.

"I received your report."

"That was fast."

"Your work is important, Doctor. Correct me if I'm wrong, but things don't look good."

"I wouldn't say that."

"No? Our drug is unstable. It's coming apart at the seams. Can't make up its mind what to do."

"It's reacting to something. Gravity, most likely."

"And the cells? How are they doing?"

"They're alive."

"How alive?"

"They're not dead."

"Not dead is good."

"I've made some adjustments. We'll know more in a few days."

"Our fate is in your hands. H82W8 is useless to me as it is."

Be patient, Gunjita wanted to say. She knew not to.

Laura Gleem smiled, as though reading her mind. "On another note, what do you think of pink?"

"Pink?"

"For the treatment center. And the personnel. The nurses and technicians."

She'd forgotten about this other plan for the station.

"The doctors, too," said Laura. "Pink with purple piping."

Gunjita was not a big fan of the color. "Sounds like a boutique."

"That's exactly what it is. A medical boutique in outer space. Shuttle up, take the cure, shuttle home. If not this cure, then another. We'll find something."

"A little holiday."

"Exactly."

"Expensive."

"More expensive not to, if your health's at stake. Future job for you, Doctor. Get this drug to work, okay?"

Not a job that particularly appealed to her, coddling and cosseting anyone, well-to-do or otherwise. As for her current job, less appealing with Laura Gleem breathing down her neck.

"I have a question for you," she said.

"Fire away."

"Pink."

"What about it?"

"Do you wear pink?"

"Do I?"

"I saw you once in person years ago. Now I just see you on-screen. I just see this . . . what everyone sees. Why's that?"

Laura stared at her. The corners of her mouth edged up. No warmth in the look, but plenty of chill.

"This object. On the asteroid. What is it?"

"I was just wondering. Maybe there's something we can do to help."

"You can help by doing your job. Now: this object."

"We're studying it."

"I've been advised to send someone. A team."

She knew what Cav would say to that. Kept her mouth shut.

"It looks like vomit," said Laura.

"I've pointed that out."

"And Dr. Cavanaugh? What does he say?"

"He has his own opinion." Let her read between the lines. Gunjita had no doubt she could.

"Of course. I look forward to hearing it."

"You will," she replied brusquely.

Laura was silent for a moment. Gunjita feared she had gone too far. Then Laura said, "It's yours for now. Keep it to yourself. No reason to alarm anybody needlessly. Understood?"

"Yes. Absolutely. I'm in full agreement."

"And don't get too distracted by it. H82W8 comes first. Prioritize, Doctor. Stay in touch."

She ended the transmission, leaving Gunjita feeling tense and manipulated. She had the urge to retaliate, which surprised her. She tried deep breathing. Then padmasana, the lotus pose, the only one she knew. Old age had made it nearly impossible, but now it was easy. Levitation, too, which up to then had eluded her.

But the knotted-up feeling persisted. Neck, shoulders, legs. Like coils of rope wound too tight, like springs about to snap. She wanted to throw something, do something. Run, punch, kick. Something physical . . . if she didn't, she was going to explode.

She and Cav used to wrestle, back in the day. A way to blow off steam after an argument, sometimes a prelude to sex. He pinned her nearly every time, his sheer size an insurmountable advantage. Now a mere shadow of himself, she could beat him easily. Turn the tables. Sit on his face.

She was tempted.

In the end she decided to take out her frustration in the Onizuka mod, which had a treadmill, bike, resistance trainer, and a VR setup that synched with each. She chose a FPS that put her in a ring, initially against a lead-footed ogre who could take a punch, working her upper body first. After that, heart, legs, and lungs, building up a sweat to the sound of her Velcro soles ripping off the belt, along with the cheers and heckles of the ringside mob. Felt better afterward, wiped herself down, PO'd a liter and a half, then returned to the observation mod. Cav hadn't budged.

"I talked to Laura Gleem."

"It moved," he said.

Stunned, she pressed her face to the glass. The Ooi looked exactly the same as before, in exactly the same position. She took a photo, compared it to an earlier one. Couldn't find a shadow of a difference.

Cav had to agree. "Interesting."

"In what way?"

"It moved, then returned to its exact original shape and position. Like a spring. As though engineered. Or preordained."

"Or imagined."

"You don't believe me."

"Let's do some tests."

"Not yet."

"When?"

"It could be dormant. Or partially dormant. If it moved once, it'll move again. We need to give it time. Maybe it needs to feel more comfortable. More secure."

The Ooi was plastered to its rock, cozy as a button. Cav

was plastered to his chair.

"Take a break," she said. "Get some rest. I'll watch. Promise. I won't miss a thing."

. . .

The next day Cav agreed to spectroscopy. Light spectroscopy first, the least destructive. According to most people, not destructive at all.

The asteroid was high in carbon, no surprise. It had carbon's distinctive black color. It also contained trace amounts of oxygen, hydrogen, phosphorus, and nitrogen, some in molecular form. They found carbon chains and rings, amino acids, hydroxyl and methyl groups, phosphates, and amines. The asteroid was a chemical smorgasbord. They learned a lot.

They learned less about the Ooi. Or rather, they learned something, possibly a great deal, but didn't know what it meant. The Ooi had similar chemical composition to the asteroid, as far as its elements were concerned. LIF showed that. But its Raman spectra, which detected atomic bonding, were difficult to interpret. They varied from scan to scan. No two readings were identical. The first showed one molecular signature, the second a slightly different one, the third slightly different yet again. Could have been due to absorption of radiation used by the tests themselves. Or to something else entirely.

What did this mean? As far as Cav was concerned, only that the Ooi defied spectroscopic definition. He could think of a number of reasons why. None of them disabused him of the notion that it was living. Its signal varied. So what? Variability was a defining feature of living systems, which characteristically showed peaks and valleys of activity, stochastic swings within a range. Not usually at the level of small molecules, but even there, conceivably. He guessed there was a pattern, which they'd observe if they waited long enough.

"We should tell Gleem," said Gunjita.

"Tell them what?"

"What we've found so far. Send them our measurements. See what they come up with."

"It's a little early for that. We've barely gotten started."

"They're waiting," she said.

"Let them."

"The Ooi isn't yours, Cav. Technically speaking, it's theirs."

"It's no one's."

"The asteroid's theirs."

"So we'll send them our analysis of it. That's what they're interested in. Can they make money from it? I'm afraid they'll be disappointed."

"We need to say something about the Ooi."

"We have nothing to say."

"How about this: we're busy. The great man is thinking. We need more time. Leave him alone."

"Perfect."

"You're living in a cave," she said. "They'll send someone if we don't communicate."

. . .

The following day they added IINS spectroscopy to their testing, repeating it three separate times, with the same confounding results. Cav wanted to do a fourth. Gunjita put her foot down.

"You love to do this," she said.

"Do what?"

"You know we're going in there."

"Eventually."

"You're procrastinating."

"Due diligence, Gunjita."

"Delayed gratification, Cav."

She was right.

"I'm suiting up," she announced.

He nodded. It was time. Fact was, he couldn't wait.

"I'll be right behind you, sweetheart," he said.

The big concern, of course, was contamination. Human beings, even freshly cleaned, plucked, shaved, deodorized, debugged, and antisepticized, were not germ-free. Germs, quasigerms, and pieces of germs in the form of embedded fragments of genetic code, and other, nonembedded pieces in free-floating form, and still others in the process of active mutation to create new germ pieces, germs of the future, lived in, on, around, and through the thing called human. A human being was fertile soil, a Garden of Eden for nonhuman organisms, simulacrum of the Earth itself, built over eons through trial and error and slow accretion of materials, including living materials. A body was a magnet for all manner of life, bringing it together, binding it energetically, holding it in balance. A laboratory for experimentation, a friendly host, a breeding ground, a passenger, as well as a carrier, and notoriously good at spreading disease.

Also good at attracting disease: life attracted life.

And good at warding it off. Repelling invasion. Usually very good at this on Earth, where the invaders, as a rule, were familiar, and used familiar tactics.

The Ooi came from outer space.

"I know what you're thinking," said Gunjita. "Please don't."

They were standing at the door to the cargo bay, suited and gloved, helmets in hand.

"Don't what?"

"Take off your helmet when we're inside. Or your gloves."

"I don't intend to."

"That's good to hear. And your contrarian streak? The side that loves to ad-lib?"

"It's under control."

"Also good."

"Honestly? I'm not worried. I don't sense we're at risk. Not bodily. But the reverse . . . if we harmed it? Unconscionable. I can't imagine anything worse. Until we know more, a lot more, I'm not willing to take that risk."

She was cheered to hear this. But like every silver lining, there was a cloud attached. What did it mean for the future of this little project of theirs, this little side job—delving into the riddle of the ages, the burning question on every stargazers' mind since the dawn of time: Are we alone in the universe, is there other life?—for one of the lead scientists to claim he had "a feeling" they weren't at risk?

Helmets on, they entered the bay. The asteroid floated a couple of feet above the floor, held in place by bungies. It was charcoal-black, its surface angular, sharp-edged, and irregular, all save one small section that looked engineered. Four narrow ledges rising not far from the Ooi, like miniature stairs. As though carved in the rock. As though purposeful.

Gunjita quickened her pace. She refused to believe it.

"Slowly," Cav whispered.

She stopped at arm's length from the pint-sized stairs, just to the right of the Ooi. Moments later, Cav joined her. They were stabilized by Velcro soles on their boots. The Ooi appeared unaware of their presence. If aware, it appeared unperturbed.

"Someone's playing a joke on us," she said.

"Mother Nature. She loves jokes."

"You think they're random?"

"Not random. But not deliberate."

"I hope not." She leaned closer. "You think the rock could fracture just like this? In just this pattern?"

Cav had his eyes on the Ooi. He suppressed the thought that it was responsible for what they were seeing.

Gunjita answered herself. "Of course it could."

He nodded.

"Big universe," she added.

"Huge."

She wasn't entirely sold. Objectivity was key. But the more she looked, the less the stairs resembled stairs, the more they flattened out, or else deepened, shifting shape, becoming other shapes, other patterns, as though her vision had become unglued.

She took a step back and blinked several times. Slowly, the stairs reconstituted themselves. But they looked ever so slightly different. The lines looked harder. The dimensions more chiseled. More muscular. As if a new way of seeing were asserting itself in her. A new spatial awareness.

Interesting.

She glanced at Cav, who was transfixed by the Ooi. She knew what he was thinking. She could tell by the rapturous look on his face. Seeing it, she understood that she'd been overly ambitious. Had asked too much of herself. Objectivity was at best an approximation. Subjectivity was impossible to fully control or suppress. Its source in this case was a photo of a snow-capped peak she'd taken years before, and which, recently, had somehow wormed its way on-screen attached to a smiling, apple-cheeked Tyrolean face urging her to book a repeat visit. She'd seen the photo that very day.

"I was thinking about that trip we took to the Alps," she said. "Do you remember? We were collecting extremophiles. A storm nearly knocked us off the mountain. Fortunately, the Swiss had conveniently carved steps into the rock face."

He remembered. "A scary experience."

"Unforgettable." In fact, she'd forgotten until the photo. A memory unburied by spam. "We see what's familiar. Experience thwarts objectivity. It interferes."

"And informs."

"Yes. Informs and interferes."

"A balance," he said. "Like everything. Take a look at this." He was pointing to an arm of the Ooi. It was shaped like a camel's hump. On the opposite side was another hump-shaped arm, slightly wider and also slightly thicker. "Symmetrical, you think?"

"Almost."

"Yes. An almost symmetry."

Symmetry implied organization, a cornerstone of life. Though not necessarily life. Atoms and molecules were extremely well organized. On a larger scale, so were galaxies.

"It's getting energy from somewhere," he said.

"That's a big leap."

"I'm assuming. From the phosphates, you think?"

What was the spectroscope seeing that he didn't? More to the point, why was he seeing the Ooi so much better than the machine? If the spectroscope was to be believed, it should have been a blur. To him it was a map, exquisitely drawn, of intrigue and mystery. Three-dimensional, maybe more. Shiny, smooth, lumpy, yellowish-green. Not large, but life came in all sizes. A speck could be a universe. Intelligence could hide in plain view.

He bent to study it closer, careful not to brush it with his helmet, wishing he could do without the helmet, stifling the urge.

Where was a HUBIE when you needed one?

He cringed at the thought, quickly suppressed it.

Turned his attention instead to the Ooi's method of staying in place. It appeared attached to the asteroid, draped across a narrow crevice. How was it attached? And why? What was the nature of the interface?

It seemed to flow over the rock, over and possibly into, as a liquid might have flowed before hardening and congealing. He imagined a connection between it and the asteroid, an interarticulation, a sharing of some sort, possibly one-directional, more likely back and forth. Perhaps it had roots. Perhaps a tube, or many tubes. Perhaps feet. A mouth? Why not? Everything needed to eat.

It feathered to an edge that was no more than one or two millimeters thick. He had to stifle another urge, this one to lift its border (if it could be lifted), peel it back, and have a peek. A terrible idea, inviting disaster. But he'd learn so much.

The lumps, for example. What were they? He had a feeling that sooner or later he'd have to find out directly, through an incision, and he cringed at this thought, too. The last thing he wanted to do was harm it. Besides, his knife-wielding days were past. As exciting as surgery had once been, he'd long since preferred a hands-on, not-in, approach.

Plus he was old, himself no stranger to the knife. He'd

been stabbed surgically on three separate occasions. Nothing major, or that he wouldn't consent to again. But each stab was a violation, shocking to the body and the spirit. The first time was the worst, each subsequent shock duller, as though he were becoming desensitized, when in fact it was the opposite. He felt more vulnerable to injury than ever, and paradoxically more resistant, as though as his outer self became frailer, his inner, truer self retreated and became harder to reach. And what could be reached was more courageous and resolute. He hoped this were so. Courage was always welcome, but never more than in old age.

The Ooi might be just as old, or older.

Did it have a dormant, cryptobiotic state? Was that what they were seeing? How had it looked and acted when young? Had it always been this shape? Had it always had lumps? There were seven of them, all small, some smooth, some chunkier.

"What do you think?" he asked Gunjita.

"A silicate, I'm guessing. Maybe a quartz of some kind."

"You're sticking to your guns."

"Nothing's changed my mind. We need a piece. Doesn't have to be big. We can probe it for biological activity."

"We have probes?"

"We do."

"Why? We don't need them. Not for the H82W8

work."

"Part of my toolkit, dear. Never leave home without them."

"You're amazing. How many?"

"A few hundred."

"Unlikely we're going to find a match."

"It's a start."

"Unreasonable to expect the same evolutionary path as Earth," he pointed out.

"I'll deep sequence it then. How's that?"

"It may not even have DNA. Probably doesn't."

"Let's find out."

"How big of a sample do we need?"

"Tiny," she said.

He stared at the Ooi. Could it be alive? If so, could it feel pain, or any sensation recognizable to a human? Would it hurt to be knifed? How would it feel being punctured, dissected, and sliced? He had no idea. But he knew how it felt to him.

"Let's hold off," he said.

"We've watched it for two days. How much longer do you plan on waiting?"

"Before cutting it? As long as I can."

"Before admitting it's a rock."

"Jury's still out. We need to run more tests."

"You're impossible, you know that?"

"I do know that. Your patience means everything."

She rolled her eyes. "What are you seeing that I'm not?"

"I don't know what I'm seeing. Honestly. I don't know what this is."

"Peas and diced chicken," she said.

"In reference to . . ."

"You asked what I thought."

"Ah. Yes. You're doubling down."

"I am. It looks like puke."

"Thank you. Very scientific."

"Inclusions, okay? Obviously."

"Mineral?"

"Yes."

He unfolded his gloved hand and held it above the Ooi. Feeling for heat, or cold, or anything. "Not organs?"

"No."

"Or organelles?"

"No. Not organs or organelles. And not symmetric, either. Randomly distributed."

"Random to us," he replied.

She gave him a look. "We don't call it science, Cav, if you keep rewriting the rules. We call it your version of things. Then it's your word versus the world. Let's avoid that. Instead, let's agree on some basic principles. Mathematics, for one. Physics. Reproducibility."

The palm of his hand had started to tingle. He checked his glove. Needed to check his skin. The Ooi, as far as he could tell, hadn't changed.

"I agree completely. We need more tests. Noninvasive ones."

They left the bay, sealed the door, removed their helmets and gloves in the airlock. The skin of his hand looked normal. He rubbed his palm.

"Something the matter?" she asked.

"It's tingling."

"Let me look."

"There's nothing to see."

She grabbed his hand, inspected it.

"It's gone now," he said.

"Put your gloves back on."

He nodded. She put hers on, too. Then the helmets, and they went back.

He repeated what he'd done, holding his hand inches above the Ooi. He had a mild age-related tremor, and the effort of keeping his hand in place accentuated it. After a while he got a cramp, along with a pins-and-needles sensation nearly identical to what he'd felt before. He switched hands, then took a break. Gunjita relieved him, cupping both her palms above the Ooi, as if it were a crystal ball.

"Anything?" he asked.

She shook her head. "You okay?"

"Just tingling a little."

"Like before?"

He didn't respond right away, working his hand. Then he said, "Yeah. More or less."

. . .

The next day they added more nondestructive tests. In medicalese these were called noninvasive, to distinguish procedures that didn't hurt, or only hurt a little, from those that hurt more, and carried more risk. The difference between, on the one hand, doing an X-ray, say, or scraping a sample of skin, or snaking a tube through the nose or the butthole, and on the other, puncturing the skin and opening the body with a scalpel. In truth, all forms of testing were invasive. This was Cav's position, and he wasn't wrong. Mass spectroscopy bombarded an object with other objects (electrons, chemicals, light), vibrational spectroscopy with infrared radiation, MRI with electromagnetism (a dangerous test if an object were metallic, unknown in this case, and therefore out of the question), ultrasound with sound waves, X-ray with ionizing radiation. The invasions were invisible but no less real. Cav worried how the Ooi would react. He worried they might harm it. An ancillary worry, they might alter it somehow, or it might alter itself in response.

Accordingly, he used the lowest possible setting on each device to begin testing, increasing only when and if it became necessary, and then by the smallest of increments. As a result, the testing lasted two full days. In the end they knew little more than when they'd started. Or rather, they knew this:

The Ooi resisted description. The infrared absorption results, like the Raman spectra, were variable and impossible to pin down. Ditto, crystallography, thermography, and CT. They couldn't say one way or another if it had an aura, and therefore how many of the seven aural layers were functional, and if it had seven layers and not eight, or twenty-eight, and how they looked, and what they did, because they didn't have an auralyzer. It hadn't made the equipment cut.

Otherwise, the station was decked to the nines. If John and Jane Q could have a Doppler in their bedroom, a chemalyzer in their bathroom, and a MRI in their closet, a state-of-the-art lab, with state-of-the-art experts, and a state-of-the-art medical boutique in the works could hardly expect less.

The ultrasound alone provided a stable image. It showed a grayish, ground glass, nonspecific matrix broken here and there by chunky inclusions.

"What the hell *is* it?" Gunjita was intrigued. She couldn't help but be. She also felt thwarted.

"A puzzle, that's what."

They were in their sleep mod, a double-wide. Venus, the Bringer of Peace, was playing. Cav was making an entry in his journal.

"I have an insane desire to charge in there and rip it off the rock," she said.

"Please don't."

"I feel like it's holding out on us. Like it might respond to more forceful measures."

He gave her a look. "I just want to touch it. I think it might respond to touch."

He was starting to get on her nerves. He sounded so tentative. So touchy-feely and irresolute. It had been two long days of testing and retesting. Hope and frustration. Talk and more talk.

"Let's wrestle," she said.

He was bigger than she was. Outweighed her by twenty kilos. This meant little to nothing in space. She was far superior to him in agility and reflexes.

She grabbed his wrists, stepped inside his leg, and pulled him toward her. He fell forward, she tucked herself into him, and the two of them somersaulted backward. They quickly struck a wall, and ping-ponged back to strike another. She was having fun, and clearly in charge.

His breath was coming in bursts.

"Give up?" she asked.

"Not on your life."

She took him through another circuit. By the end of it he was gasping.

"Now? Ready to wave the white flag?"

He had a snappy rejoinder, but it died on his lips. He felt faint. His heart was skipping beats, like a drunk doing hopscotch. It was scary, and definitely not good.

"Cav? What's the matter? Cav? Talk to me."

He heard the worry in her voice, but it was distant. *She* was distant. A darkness was descending. The world was slipping away.

Then suddenly, sharply, it was back.

Gunjita was on full alert.

"I'm okay," he assured her.

"Don't lie."

"No, really. I'm fine."

She narrowed her eyes.

He drew a deep breath, exhaled. "I had a thought. Before I was ruthlessly assaulted. All these nonresults. Maybe it's deliberate. Intentional."

"What just happened? You looked like you were on the way out."

He waved her off. "What if it *is* communicating? Communication by noncommunication. Silence by design."

"Enough. Please. Stop."

"There's a pattern. There's got to be a pattern."

She slapped him, then pulled down his pants and grabbed his cock.

Stunned, he looked down. She was holding it like a bludgeon.

"Easy does it," he said.

"Are you going to fuck me or not?"

Another shock. The old Gunjita made her desires known differently.

Turned out the old Gunjita had different desires. He felt stretched, like a hamstring. Not a bad experience.

Not bad at all.

Afterward, she floated above him, pupils wide, hair a thick black tangle, brain on fire.

"What if we made it a smell?"

"It being?"

"The catastrophe alarm. What if we linked the warning cascade with the olfactory system?"

He was also floating, on the proverbial post-fuck cloud. It was all he could do to reply. "What if?"

"Wouldn't even have to be unpleasant. As long as it got your attention. A pheromone, say. A sex pheromone. What's a bigger attention-getter than that?"

He had to agree. He was swimming in her scent. It—she—had taken him prisoner. Taken him by storm.

"Perfect."

"You couldn't care less."

"Not true."

"You're not listening."

"I'm intoxicated. I want to bottle you."

"I've got a better idea."

"What could be better than that?"

"Let's wrestle again."

His eyes widened.

"No? Not up to it?"

"Give me a minute."

"Poor baby. I wore you out."

He couldn't deny it. He was spent, and had never felt better. His dopey smile told the happy story, as his eyelids drifted closed.

All at once, she was alone. She felt restless and far from satisfied, far from done. She wanted more, but of what she wasn't sure. Sex was fun, and she'd always loved his body. All her life she'd had an appetite for large men. Now, strangely, his size seemed excessive and faintly repulsive, an overindulgence, like an extra plate of food when she was already full.

She wasn't full, but more of him wasn't the answer. This came as a surprise to her, as did her budding discontent.

"You've only yourself to blame," she said.

"What's that?"

"Don't you want to be young? Or do you, but not with

me? Is that what this is?"

"Only with you."

"Then do it."

He opened his eyes. "I already agreed."

"Under duress. To shut me up."

"As soon as we get back."

"So you say."

"I will. I promise. Consider it done."

And if he didn't? What then?

"It'll be done when it's done," she said.

"Can we talk about something else for a minute?"

"Do I have a choice?"

"I want to try some provocative tests. Bright lights, loud noise, pressure variation. See if we can get our unknown visitor to respond."

"Okay. Good. And then? If it doesn't?"

"Take the next step."

"We need a sample."

"First I want to touch it. With my bare skin. I want to smell it."

She knew he did. She did, too. "Big risk."

"You don't even believe it's living."

"I don't. You're right. But a tiny percentage of me isn't sure. I have you to thank for that."

"I'll sterilize my hands. I'll exhale into a tube. I'll make sure not to sneeze."

"You could still contaminate it."

"I could. It's true."

"And the risk to you?"

This was the tricky part. He was willing to take the risk. He wasn't afraid. But he wasn't alone. If something *did* go wrong, if it *did,* Gunjita would be left holding the bag.

"I've been thinking," he said.

"You're always thinking."

"We can eliminate the risk."

"How?"

He hesitated.

"Spit it out."

It wasn't easy, but he took a stab. Started with a preamble, then backtracked, preambling the preamble, laying the groundwork, which couldn't be rushed, was occasionally hard to follow, and went on forever.

"You're making me nervous," she said.

This was plain to see, and the opposite of what he intended.

Then it hit her. "You can't be serious."

"You won't have a dead body on your hands."

"No. Absolutely not."

"Try to be open-minded."

"Are you crazy? It should have never happened. It was wrong from the start. It was sick. Nothing's changed."

"We didn't make them."

"*You* didn't."

"You didn't, either."

"I set the stage."

"You're too hard on yourself."

"What does that mean? I accept responsibility for the role I played. That doesn't mean I need to rub my face in it."

"If it wasn't you, it would have been someone else."

"That's enough."

"It *wasn't* you."

"I said enough."

"I have to smell it, Gunjita. I have to touch it. You of all people should understand."

"I do understand. But my answer is no."

"Please reconsider."

"And if I don't?"

"Just do."

The air between them thickened.

A thought occurred to her, darkening her face. "Are you blackmailing me?"

He didn't reply.

"You are, aren't you?"

She was furious, though in a way she had herself to blame. She had opened the door to him, ushered him into the world of smell and all things related. A true believer, she had made him one, too.

"This is fucked," she fumed.

"One other thing. I want to look underneath it. Peel it back if we can. If we can't, I want to look inside."

Finally. Some good news. It was what she'd been wanting from the start.

"You're ready to cut into it?"

"Not me. Look at these hands." They shook like a martini.

"You want me to do it? Fine."

"You're a researcher, Gunji."

"You've noticed."

"You've got great hands. Great hand-eye coordination. Great technique."

"But?"

"Mice, rats, rabbits . . . there's no one better. But I'm thinking someone with a slightly different take on things. Someone geared to preserving life. Not so accustomed to sacrifice as the end result."

"You want a surgeon."

"I do."

Not the strangest request, considering that he'd once been one himself.

"Does Gleem know?"

"They do. I made the request."

"Did they agree?"

"They did. Laura Gleem personally. Turns out she

knows the surgeon I have in mind. The two of them have had dealings in the past."

"What sort of dealings?"

"No idea."

"Who is she?"

"He. An old colleague of mine. Yours, too."

She felt a quickening inside. Touch of fire, flood of ice. "You're kidding, right?"

"I'm not."

"Are you out of your mind?"

"He's the best."

She couldn't believe what she was hearing. Who *was* this man lying next to her? What could he possibly be thinking? How could he be so dense?

The more important question, and the one that wormed its way into her brain: Why hadn't he consulted her first?

–FOUR–

> He hovered, and stayed still, striking on the
> crumbling columns of air . . . fixed like a barb
> in the blue flesh of sky . . . turned towards the
> ground and . . . for a thousand feet he fell . . .
> and another thousand feet . . . but now he fell
> sheer, shimmering down through dazzling sun-
> light, heart-shaped, like a heart in flames.*

The cliff was several hundred meters high, and from a distance appeared unclimbable. Dashaud knew from experience that this wasn't necessarily true. From a distance the
great Vatnajökull looked like a cozy white blanket, when
in fact it was a minefield of crevasses, icefalls, and sudden,
blinding storms.

There were small clumps of green and some stunted

---

* From *The Peregrine,* by J. A. Baker.

shrubs scattered on the cliff, meaning there was soil. Cracks and ledges to hold the soil, meaning potential hand-and footholds. A large colony of fulmars nested on the cliff, but they had bred, and were gone. He wouldn't be disturbing them, or the other way around.

The cliff had been a lifelong dream of his. It spoke to him in the language of dreams, larger than life, unreal, seductive, forbidding. He'd been wanting to climb it since boyhood, but one thing or another had gotten in the way. When he finally found the time, was finally ready, he couldn't do it. He was old, and physically incapable of something so arduous and demanding. Now he was young again, and could do anything he wanted.

He crossed the road, then picked his way through a field of weathered basalt to the face. He saw a faint trail and took it. When it petered out, he blazed his own trail, which quickly steepened. He passed an abandoned fulmar nest made of grass. Then another in a shallow rock depression. An unseasonably late-to-migrate bird glided by, squawked at him, then disappeared.

The climb grew steeper and more difficult, but his arms and legs were strong, and his balance, a must, gymnastic. He had his father's Nordic build, long limbed and wiry, and his mother's sturdiness and endurance, and was halfway up the face before he had to stop to catch his breath.

Below him, stretching east as far as he could see, was a narrow strip of lush green farmland, bracketed between glacial moraines and the windswept sea. He could just make out the red-topped silo of his grandparents' ancient horse and sheep farm, where he'd spent much of his youth. To the west was the Gray Lagoon, fed by melt from one of Vatnajökull's once mighty tongues, now thinned and shrunken. The lagoon, by contrast, was vast, as large as it had ever been, home to an equally vast quantity and diversity of brackish life.

This pleased him, and he was already pleased: with the climb, with his fine new body, with his supple, firing-on-all-cylinders, ready-for-anything brain. The world was not just a beautiful place, it was a playground, or anything else a man with his gifts dared it to be.

He felt a mild breeze on his face. He wore gloves, not for warmth, but for protection. Since his recent enhancement he was careful to keep his hands covered at nearly all times. He'd added a second layer for the climb, and on a whim removed both.

His fingertips seemed to waken. They whispered to him of a hidden world, swarming and newly minted. The breeze was like a chorus of secrets. He noticed subtle variations in its pressure—peaks, lulls, eddies—that translated sometimes into words (swift, strong, retreating), sometimes sound (warble, bellow, screech), mostly neither, but rather the pleasant, informative, highly personal, and often electric feeling that came from being touched. Present previously, now so much richer and more complex.

He touched his lips, traced their faint corrugations, felt their turgor: firm but not too firm, pliant but not too much of that. He nudged a blade of grass, aware of its own pressure. He could feel it in the way it resisted and opposed his applied force, stubbornly but easily overwhelmed. A friendly, compliant blade, eminently floppy; a pushover, though not to a small ant that was climbing on one of its neighbors. To the ant the blade was strength itself, bending only the slightest amount, and springing quickly back to attention when the ant moved on.

The world was governed by touch, by feel, by push and push back, weight and counterweight, resistance and accommodation. He was aware of this as never before. There was a constant undercurrent of motion surrounding him, with a language all its own; a shifting, speechless tongue, perhaps the most ancient one of all. It was smooth, acrobatic, choppy, graceful, precarious, and it filled him with awe. His merkelized, piezo-powered fingertips understood it instinctively. They were his eyes, ears, nose, tongue, but he had to be careful. They could be damaged by overuse.

Any sense could be. Overstimulation sooner or later

led to exhaustion. There was only so much information a body—and any part of a body—could absorb before shutting down and signing off. Recovery was the rule, but not always.

Hence the double pair of gloves, which blunted sensation and protected him. He was not about to squander his gift.

Not everyone was so prudent.

He'd once had a patient who, first juve, had his vision enhanced. Ponied up, took the risk. The result was beyond his wildest expectations. What he saw, in his words, was "unbelievable," "indescribable," "kaleidoscopic" . . . and "nonstop." He couldn't turn his eyeballs off. Closed his lids, and the film kept running: real images, synthetic images, phantom ones, his retina working 'round the clock. An embarrassment of riches, a bombardment, an enfilade, until at length he lost his sight. Couldn't see a thing. Blinded by extravagance and overabundance.

Had no choice but to swap his retina out for a new one: standard issue, boilerplate, unenhanced. Solved half the problem. Sought out Dashaud to solve the other half, which rested not in his eyes but in the brain behind them—the optic nerve, geniculate bodies, and visual cortex—which had also been damaged by overuse. These were the source of the ghost and phantom images, the hallucinatory misinformation and random visual events.

Their repair involved some extremely delicate surgery, which Dashaud happened to be doing at the time.

He no longer did this surgery. There was less and less brain surgery being done all the time. Less surgery all around. More bio interventions, letting cells and parts of cells do the repair and cleanup themselves.

Surgeons were a dying breed.

About time, some people said. Dinosaurs. Butchers.

Until you needed one.

The good ones still had work. Still had a place.

Dashaud Mikelson was a good one. And now better than ever.

But not if he blew out his sense of touch. Who would come to a surgeon whose fingers were numb?

He slipped his gloves back on.

The inner glove was made of Pakkiflex†, and was like a second skin. The outer glove was leather: tough and grained. He resumed his climb, secure in the knowledge his hands were protected. He planned to summit, then take the backside down, which was a longer route, but more gently sloped. Descending the cliff itself

---

†   Robert Fairchild and Julian Taborz's brainchild accounted for 38 percent of the global market in responsive sheathing material. Current data compiled and reported by Blumlein et al, in *The Roberts: A Twenty-Year Follow-Up*.

would be quicker but dangerous.

The lone fulmar reappeared, and dove at him, coming close to impaling his head before veering off. It squawked and dove again, hovered, then deposited itself on a nearby rock, and proceeded to read him the riot act. He soon discovered why.

Huddling in a shallow saucer of grass was another fulmar. A male, and obviously unwell.

He stopped immediately, crouched down, and held that position. The female fulmar squawked, flapped its wings, and shifted uneasily. The male made not a peep. Its eyes were clamped shut. It was shivering.

Dashaud removed his gloves and inched a hand toward the bird. He felt vibrations in the air before even touching the creature. He felt much more when he laid his palm gently on its back: a huffing and puffing, an ebb and flow, a back and forth, but something more purposeful, too, like a tug-of-war, with life on one side, death on the other. Death appeared to have the upper hand.

Instinctively, he enfolded the trembling bird in his palms.

Its mate eyed him uneasily.

Fulmars mated for life. If the male died, the female would be a widow. Her mate's death would be the signal; she'd know widowhood by the presence of his lifeless body. If Dashaud took him away in an effort to save him, she'd have a widow's life without knowing how or why. Without certainty. She might wonder: was he still alive? Doubt might gnaw at her peanut-sized brain.

A gnawed-at brain, whatever the size, was the source of countless troubles. Dashaud had taken a solemn oath to cause as few as possible. He could leave the dying bird, and let nature take its course. Finish his climb, his ambition since childhood. He could see the summit from where he crouched.

Any hope of saving the poor creature rested on doing something soon. He peered down the way he'd come: the face was nearly sheer, the drop hundreds of feet and precipitous. It had been steep getting up, but it would be steeper going down. Always steeper and riskier descending.

He loved life. How could you not? And fulmars were plentiful.

What should he do?

He thought of Cav, his friend and mentor, whom he admired above all men, and would soon be seeing in the flesh. Cav would be slow to intervene. He would wait and observe.

He was waiting now. For what, he wasn't sure.

"A sign? An epiphany?"

They had spoken not two days earlier. Pleased to hear from his orbiting pal, Dashaud had become concerned when the conversation took a turn.

A dark one, in his opinion. Suicide was dark.

"You're depressed," he said. It was the first thing that came into his head.

Cav considered this. "Am I? I don't feel depressed. I feel quite sane."

"You want to end your life prematurely. You want to do something totally unnecessary. And not just unnecessary, but damaging. Hurtful. Harmful. How can that be sane?"

"It's my life," said Cav.

"You took an oath to do no harm."

"It's a paradox, isn't it? A thorny riddle."

"It's not a riddle at all."

"A dilemma then."

"No harm includes no harm to yourself."

"Does it? I'm not so sure. And what constitutes harm? What I'm contemplating feels more positive. More an acknowledgement. An acceptance."

"You ask too many questions. You spin them out of thin air. You love to stir things up."

"I'm a troublemaker?"

"Yes."

"But am I crazy? That's the question. Tell me the truth."

Dashaud had no trouble with this. "Yes."

"In what way? Be precise."

"You're bullheaded. Argumentative. You love to provoke. You go off on tangents."

"Guilty as charged. But crazy?"

"You make *me* crazy."

Cav grinned. "It's good to see you, my friend."

"Likewise. Though I'm not thrilled with the circumstances. Please tell me it's just talk."

Cav deflected the question. Enough for now. "You juved."

"You knew I was going to."

"How was it?"

"Not bad. Fine. Easy." Not true, but considering the topic of conversation, Cav hardly needed to hear it. "I feel good."

"You look good."

"You look old."

"I am."

"How's your ticker?"

Cav shrugged.

"It could be brand new."

"Understood. And then?"

"Sixty more years," said Dashaud.

"Of what? Doing the same thing over again. Looking in the same mirror day after day. You reach a point of diminishing returns."

"Not my experience."

"True nonetheless."

"That's possible. Also possible: you're full of it."

"I'm not afraid of dying," said Cav.

Dashaud was neither surprised nor particularly impressed. He'd seen his share of dying; his line of work guaranteed he'd see more. More men and women who met death fearfully, but many more than that who, for better or worse, welcomed it.

"Good for you," he replied. "But this isn't about that. It's about taking your life."

"It's about taking control of my life."

"By committing suicide."

"By letting nature run its course."

"You know something, Cav?"

"What's that?"

"I hate talking to you."

Cav threw up his hands. "I understand completely. I get tired of listening to myself. Days go by when the only thing I wish for is silence."

To Dashaud, an ominous choice of word. "Do you have an actual plan?"

"A number."

"Seriously?"

"I'm mulling things over."

"Yes or no?"

"Am I serious? Yes. Am I ready to pull the trigger? No."

"So there's hope."

"Either way. Yes. Always."

Dashaud felt better. Worried, yes, who wouldn't be worried, but not quite so alarmed. This was a Cav he knew. A familiar Cav, tossing out an idea, inviting reaction. The discussion could last for months. Years. Humor sometimes helped. Close-mindedness rarely did.

"So. Two and out."

"It's an option."

"It's a waste, you ask me. But you're not."

"Helps to talk."

"Glad you called."

The two of them fell silent.

At length Cav cleared his throat. "There's something else. I've got a favor to ask."

"Tell me."

"You can start by describing this enhancement of yours."

"I'm still getting used to it." He described his experience so far. "Sometimes it feels like a whole new sense. Not merely an improved one. I recognize things that I couldn't. That didn't exist to me."

"Such as?"

"Pressure gradients. Vibrations. Big and little energy fluctuations. Nothing's at rest, Cav. Nothing. Everything's in motion."

"I believe it."

"Motion and countermotion. Back and forth. Peaks and valleys. Steady streams. Though mostly not steady."

"Transitioning. Balancing."

"Yes."

"The song of life."

"Not just life. Everything."

Cav leaned in excitedly, until his face took up the whole screen. "Can you distinguish living from nonliving?"

"Easily. Who can't?"

"There's some disagreement on board." He explained what they had, and what they'd done. What they knew, and what they didn't.

"You believe it's alive," said Dashaud.

"Not only alive, but a new form of life. One we've never seen."

"Sentient?"

"Unknown."

He had a look. Dashaud had seen it before.

"I need you here," said Cav.

"When?"

"As soon as possible."

"How?"

"It's been arranged."

"Excellent."

"But first there's an errand I want you to run."

. . .

It turned out to be a blockage in its gullet, a little external growth of tissue that closed it like a purse, making the bird unable to swallow. Dashaud removed it that evening, in a delicate operation made easy by his magical fingers. He released it the next day at the cliff, the female nowhere in sight. As he walked away, it took to the air, wheeled in a lazy circle, as if to test its wings, then headed out to sea. The day was overcast. The water, gunmetal gray. A mist hung in the distance, and before long its small white solitary body was swallowed by it.

The following day he left Iceland and flew to Denver, got a car and drove south along the Front Range, then farther south, then west. Cav had given him an address outside a town called Cinder Knife. The way it worked, he'd talked to someone, Cav had, who'd talked to someone else, who'd talked to a third person, who'd contacted the seller and confirmed. Making the trail all but impossible to follow, in the event someone got a stick up their ass.

The town was one block long and all boarded up, swept by the gritty desert sand and mummified by the hot, dry air. It could have been a hundred years old.

Could have been two hundred. Dashaud blew through it, then had to slow down as he wound his way across the high plateau, past scrub, black rock, and a labyrinth of rutted dirt and gravel roads to a mailbox that sat atop a twisted and charred juniper stump. Behind it a tall pole with a security cam. Beside it a crushed rock driveway. He drove to the end of the driveway and got out.

The sun nearly knocked him over. The heat was brutal. He got his cap, then looked around.

In front of him was the back end of a double-wide, with a short flight of stairs leading to a door. Off to the side was another, larger building with cinder-block walls and a corrugated sheet metal roof, topped by a swivel-mounted cam. The place belonged to two brothers, he'd been told. One was a successful writer who had died some years earlier, under somewhat shady circumstances. Suspicion had fallen on the surviving brother, but nothing could be nailed down. In the end no charges were filed.

The brother was said by some to be reclusive and misanthropic, though others pointed out that three-quarters of the local citizenry fit that description. Chances were he was perfectly likable, to someone anyway. He made a living designing and building things: water towers, personalized surveillance equipment, computer arrays, and, most important for the purpose of Dashaud's errand, cooling systems.

He materialized silently, like an apparition. He was wearing jeans, sneakers, and a holstered pistol. Asked for ID.

Dashaud handed it over.

He studied it, then gestured. "Your cap. Off."

Dashaud removed it. Got his photo taken for at least the third time. SOP, he guessed, though his size and the color of his skin still made some people nervous. Not many, not now, not here in the twenty-second century, what some were calling the Age of Yes, Finally. The Age of About Time. The Age of Long Overdue.

The guy flicked his eyes from the fish-eye nestled in his palm to his visitor, awaiting confirmation. He had deep-set eyes, a wiry frame, and a pendulous beard. At length he gave a nod and pocketed the device.

"You're the guy who made them," he said.

"One of the guys. There was a team."

"You headed it."

He'd been criticized and demonized in the past, more times than he could count. Used to defend himself, in shouting matches if necessary. Finally learned to thicken his skin and not rise to the bait. Ignorant people didn't come to learn. Hypocrites didn't want to be educated. All they wanted was to point the finger of blame.

"Long time ago. Unique situation."

"You did what you were told."

"I did what was right."

"You volunteered."

Actually, he was picked. "Yes."

"No questions asked."

The guy had it all figured out. Dashaud had heard it a hundred times before. He glanced at the holster, which appeared to be homemade, then the gun.

Cav had mentioned the man was eccentric. He'd said nothing about the prospect of being shot.

"You alive during the Hoax?" he asked.

A dip of the chin.

"Then you know how it was."

"Not much different today."

An interesting observation. Save for two small clouds, three buzzards, and a faraway plane, the sky was clear. Not a thing in it you wouldn't expect. Had been that way for over fifty years. Smart money said it would stay that way. You had your skeptics, naturally. Your holdouts. Your crazy-ass contrarians.

"You know something I don't?" he asked, hazarding a friendly grin.

The guy's eyes narrowed. His finger twitched.

"Let me try that again."

"You're making a joke." He looked bewildered. Slowly, comprehension spread across his face.

Next thing Dashaud knew, his hand was being gripped and eagerly pumped up and down.

"Cantrell. Abel. It's an honor to meet you. Didn't recognize you at first."

"Do we know each other?"

"Skin color didn't match. You look lighter than your photo. Threw me off. You know how it is. Can't be too careful. Let me show you around."

Dashaud turned out to be something of a hero of his. Once over the recog hump, he got the red carpet treatment, beginning with the house, then the grounds, an acre and a half of high desert with an unobstructed view of more of the same, all the way to the horizon. The tour ended in the other building on the property, the workshop, which was the jewel box, and dwarfed the house.

Big, airy, neat, and bright, with four large stainless-steel tables on the ground floor, two more on the upper, equipment of every sort hanging on pegboards, resting on overhead racks, standing on edge against walls, and hidden in meticulously labeled cabinets and drawers. On one of the tables was an open metal box stuffed with wires and circuit boards, with a sleeve jutting out that connected to a jointed arm that ended in a cup with a rubber ball. (A game of catch? Batting practice? His host didn't seem the type. Of fetch? More likely, but with what? He'd seen no pets.) On another was version 3.4

of his patented, custom-made, automated feline feeder, adapted to the outdoors to service ferals, and equipped with mo detection and facial analytics to exclude skunks, raccoons, opossums, rats, and other party crashers. It was working well except for the opossums, which were somehow eluding the software.

"Maybe they're playing possum," suggested Dashaud.

Cantrell gave him a look. "What else would they be playing?"

Industrious, inventive, and literal to a fault. Dashaud loved the guy. He was there for a reason but didn't mind putting it off.

Cantrell moved the metal box, then returned to the table, which was bolted to the concrete floor. He pulled out his handheld, entered a code, and a tawny, green-eyed tabby appeared on-screen. He touched one of the tabby's eyes, swept his finger to an ear, then a paw, then repeated this in reverse. After the third time the tabby mewed, and scampered offscreen. Cantrell stepped back. Four previously hidden seams appeared in the floor, which opened like a door. The table swung up and over to reveal a set of stairs.

"My hideaway," said Cantrell.

"They're down there?"

"Safe and sound. Go ahead. Light'll come on by itself."

He hadn't set eyes on one for years. Had made his

peace. You did what you did. In hindsight everyone was guilty of something.

He started down.

The light came on.

Water under the bridge.

He reached the bottom.

The losers were the ones who never did anything.

The room was cave-like. A refrigeration unit sat on the floor in front of him, connected via hose to a cupboard-sized stainless-steel panel mounted on a wall.

They were in the panel. Had to be.

His heart was in his throat.

Cantrell was right behind him. "Excited?"

He shrugged.

"Guess that's a yes. Let's not prolong the suspense."

He strode forward, put his hand on the panel, then paused, prolonging it. "Not that there is any. Don't get the wrong idea. They're in tip-top shape."

"I'm sure they are."

"You bet they are. Couldn't be better." He ran his finger along the panel's edge with evident affection. "I check them regularly. I have a system. You don't want to take too long. Don't want to risk disturbing them."

One by one he released the panel's clamps, and slowly removed the cover. There were three of them nestled behind a thick plate of glass, curled like commas, barely touching, suspended in translucent fluid, with no room to spare.

Dashaud's stomach lurched.

His mind rebelled. He took a step back, repulsed.

What had he done?

And yet.

When was progress ever black and white? How else did men and women advance?

They were hideous. Appalling.

But beautiful, too.

Beautifully conceived, designed, and executed. He couldn't forget the day they came to life. His pride and joy.

His creations.

Cantrell was champing at the bit. "So? What do you think?"

"They're hibernating?"

"Of course."

He had a welter of emotions, which he cloaked behind a professional veneer. "Fully functional?"

"Will be, once they're thawed out."

Naturally, he'd say this. "How cold do you keep them?"

"Cold as I can without harming them. Just above freezing. Never lower than point-three, higher than point-seven. Narrow range."

"You made the cooling system?"

"All of it. Cooling, housing, electronics."

"Impressive."

"The premade stuff is junk. Even the good stuff is never quite what you need. Doing it yourself saves time in the end. Saves money." He touched the glass, traced the outline of one of them. "I'm quite fond of this particular system."

Dashaud leaned in to study it closer. An intricate puzzle of hoses, filters, gauges, housing, and circuitry. Ingenious and original, though his eye, understandably, kept wandering to the living contents.

"It's a work of art," he said.

"Does the job," replied Cantrell, basking.

"How long have you had them?"

"Ten years next month."

"Like this?"

"Pretty much."

"Long time."

"They're worth holding onto."

Not what he was getting at. "How do we know they're still good?"

"It's a good system. Works on mice, rabbits, monkeys. All your basic vertebrates. No reason it's not going to work with these. Would have been easier if you'd engineered them with an eye toward longevity. But they'll be fine. Warm 'em up, you'll see."

He replaced the cover, clamped it down, and ushered Dashaud upstairs. In the workshop he pointed out a similar-looking panel, this one portable.

"Longevity wasn't our aim," Dashaud replied defensively. "Our concerns were more immediate."

"Knee-jerk," said Cantrell.

"Urgent."

"Ecologically unsound."

"How so?"

"You made them disposable."

"Readily available and easy to use," said Dashaud. The description the makers preferred.

"Not saying it was a flaw in the design. In the planning, more like. Strictly short-term. Not seeing the forest, et cetera, et cetera. What governments do."

"What's the forest?"

"You're here, aren't you?"

"Completely different reason. There's no threat, real or otherwise. No danger. No anything."

Cantrell wasn't buying it. "You're just spending money for the fun of it? You're a collector maybe? A dealer in rare things?"

He was fishing, and wasn't far off. In a way they did belong in a museum.

"Research," said Dashaud.

"On what?"

"Classified. Sorry."

Cantrell nodded knowingly, a gleam in his eye, then escorted his guest out of the workshop. In the house he offered him shark and Aquavit.

Dashaud was touched: the guy had done his research, and gone out of his way. But shark? In the desert? A thousand miles from any ocean, not to mention the chill waters of Iceland, where proper sharks were caught, beheaded, fermented, and hung to dry. Nothing could touch them for flavor and taste. He'd been spoiled by perfection, and took a pass.

"A drink would do nicely."

Cantrell poured them each a glass. Dashaud removed his gloves.

"Something wrong with your hands?"

"Not a thing." He explained his recent augmentation.

"Nice. So now you're a super surgeon. I guess that's what it takes these days."

"Takes?"

"To hold the line. Keep the robots at bay. Personally, I'd take one of them over a human. No offense."

"None taken."

"Better outcomes. Steadier hands."

Dashaud glanced at his own. Steady as a rock.

"Had one once," said Cantrell. "Did a great job."

"How was its bedside manner?"

"Very professional."

Dashaud could imagine. Now and then he toyed with becoming a veterinarian. Maybe the time had arrived.

"Can we get down to business?"

"Sure thing."

He was surprised to learn that Cantrell did not own the HUBIES‡. Had somehow missed the law declaring that ownership was a crime, while using was not. A strange disconnect, not unheard of in the annals of ethics and morality. Use alone was problematic for the vast majority of people. There was a fine line, some said no line at all, between use and abuse.

"So what does this mean? You're lending them?"

"Sharing," said Cantrell. "Passing them along."

"For a price."

"Cost plus expenses."

"No profit?"

"Lots of profit. Just not monetary."

Dashaud was pleasantly surprised. "That's very gen-

---

‡   A word of apocryphal origin. 1. An acronym for Hybrid Usable Body in Idiosyncratic Encephaloid State; alternatively, HUman Boosted Inhalation Experiment; 2. An insult, a slur; 3. A tribute, an accolade, an expression of esteem, as in "She hubied herself for the cause"; 4. Brainless and stupid; 5. An anagram for SHIEBU, goddess of perfume and good deeds; 6. A portmanteau of "hubris" and "boobie."

erous of you."

"I have what I need. As long as I can keep inventing things. Making them, then making them better. Doing my part. Giving progress a nudge. Step by step. Circuit by circuit. Forward, out of the dark ages, into the new age."

"What's the new age?"

"Science, Doctor. Intelligence. Rational thinking. Our age. Yours and mine."

Dashaud raised his glass. "To intelligence."

"So you're using them for research," said Cantrell. "I won't ask what, but I'm curious. Does Dr. Gharia happen to be involved?"

"Gunjita Gharia?" He kept his voice level.

"That's the one. Your old boss."

"I haven't spoken to her in nearly a century."

"Really? A whole century?"

"Half a century. Fifty years at least."

"You worked in her lab."

"Briefly."

"You left."

"People do. It's expected. This was all very long ago." He was ready to move on.

But Cantrell had his teeth in it. "What was she like?"

"I barely remember. Smart. Successful."

"Like you."

"It was that kind of lab. Competitive. Highly prized.

People killed to get into it."

"Was it hard? Working side by side with her? Elbow to elbow. Two superstars, sharing the spotlight."

"I was her student. Hardly a superstar. She mentored me."

Cantrell nodded. His attention seemed to wander.

"I worked in a lab once," he said. "I had a mentor, too. He stole my ideas. When I complained, he got rid of me."

"I'm sorry to hear that."

"I got blacklisted."

"How awful."

"Is that what happened to you?"

"Not at all."

Cantrell gave him a sly, conspiratorial look, as though he recognized a kindred spirit, a comrade in arms. "She got rid of you, didn't she?"

Dashaud was speechless.

"We're not so different," Cantrell added.

Dashaud felt otherwise, as though a gauntlet had been tossed. "I got an offer from another lab. A very generous offer. She told me to take it. She was doing her job."

"Told you, or asked you? Forced you maybe?"

"She guided me. That's what mentors do."

"I was told, too. I wasn't asked. I wasn't thanked. I was coerced."

For Dashaud, an old wound, long since healed. He'd

hated her for a time, but for a much longer time had understood the wisdom in what she had done, and admired her for it.

He would not stand idly by while her reputation was dragged through the mud.

"She gave me an option."

"The HUBIE lab?"

"Wasn't called that then. But yes. There was a core group. It was a good move."

"Good? Career, Dashaud. Career. May I call you Dashaud?"

"It was a long time ago."

"Best thing that could have happened. Trust me on this."

"Look. Abel. May I call you Abel?"

"My friends call me Spud."

"Spud then."

"Like the potato. I built a satellite when I was a kid. A little one, with a tiny hollow space inside. Named it Sputnik, in honor of . . . well, you know what. Later on, I changed the name, in honor of its first payload. Know what it was?"

"A potato chip."

"How'd you guess?"

"Listen, Spud. Just to be perfectly clear. I've got no ax to grind. No grievance. Dr. Gharia's the best there is. She's in a class by herself. I've got nothing but respect for her."

Cantrell looked like the cat who swallowed the canary. "Your secret's safe with me."

"What secret? There is no secret."

Cantrell made the motion of zipping his lips.

Dashaud felt the blood rise. He had an urge to re-arrange the man's face. This came as a surprise to him, as the days of uncontrolled impulses and outbursts were behind him. Far behind, or so he thought.

Cantrell was not a small man, but Dashaud Mikelson towered over him, and was half again as broad. His fists were like hams. His chest and biceps strained against the seams of his shirt.

He eyed the man, considering his options. Age and experience had taught him the value of restraint. Now he was young, with a young man's sense of indignation and urgency, and a young man's refusal to be straitjacketed.

He raised his hands, feeling mighty and righteous, intent on wringing the man's neck.

Cantrell froze, then went for his gun. Quick, but not quick enough. Dashaud got to him first.

It was over in a second.

"Hey!" Cantrell yelped. "You're crushing me."

It was true. Dashaud had him pinned in a fierce, manly, beefcake embrace.

"Let me go!"

Dashaud released him. "So how did it taste?"

Cantrell gave him a wary look. "How did what taste?"

"The chip. When it got back."

Puzzlement. Suspicion.

Dashaud grinned. "Crisp?"

"Is this a joke?"

"Salty?"

"You're messin' with me."

"Cosmic?"

Cantrell's wariness deepened. All at once he broke into a grin. Then a laugh. Here was the brother he'd never had. Fate, or foresight, had brought them together. The HUBIES, whom he'd faithfully nursed, were theirs together. He and Dashaud were their custodians. Their guardians. He and Dashaud: inextricably bound.

"Out of this world," he said.

–FIVE–

. . . I may have seemed somewhat strange
caring in my own time for living things
*with no value that we know . . . **

Human beings were not meant to float, so naturally everyone wanted to, Cav included. You could do it on Earth with injectable micropackets of supercharged helium. He'd tried these on a couple of occasions. What he got was a roller coaster ride. One moment up (as it were), then up higher, then flat on his back. He preferred something smoother and more predictable.

He'd dreamed about a voyage into space since boyhood. It was relatively easy to book a trip, which was not to say cheap. Somehow he'd never gotten around to it. Now here he was, living the dream, but late in the game,

---

*   From *The Blind Seer of Ambon,* by W. S. Merwin.

on the downslope of life, well past his prime. A missed opportunity, and a reason for regret.

But there was no regret, and in fact, he felt the opposite. This *was* his opportunity, and it couldn't have come at a better time.

He hurt. Knees, feet, back, neck . . . the joints ground down by a lifetime of gravity. Joint replacement, once popular, now superseded by juvenation, was obsolete, a footnote in history. His pain was not terrible, but it was frequent. Occasionally, it would sharpen, and he would gasp, or freeze.

He was hardly alone in this. Soreness, achiness, little stabs and embarrassments were universal in his age group. A fact of life.

But not in space. Being weightless robbed gravity of its teeth. Bone no longer gnashed against bone. Nerves were no longer pinched. Pain went from a roar, or a dull roar, to a whisper, and often to silence. A truly liberating experience.

Liberation came at a price, however, as other age-related problems, previously overshadowed, were now freed to make their presence known. Eyes, bladder, balance, concentration. His wonky heart. Amazing all the ways a body could fall apart. Equally, or more amazing, all the ways it didn't, how well it worked, and for how long.

He loved being weightless; floating not so much. It was counterintuitive, and made him uneasy, as though his body knew it wasn't right. He'd stuck a tall stool in front of the Ooi for this reason, anchoring it to the floor. Nothing he liked better than to sit on it, strap himself down, and let his mind drift.

He was sitting now. Bouncing thoughts off the Ooi. Letting them fall where they may. Keeping all channels open.

Death was certain. There was no denying it. It went hand in hand with life.

He had seen his share of dying people. All ages, all walks, all faiths, all stripes. For some of them it appeared to be a momentous event, of the greatest significance. For others, ordinary, even mundane.

He was curious about this. The two experiences appeared so different, so polarized. He wasn't worried. He believed that all would be well, that his body would take care of itself. That after three billion years, life knew how to handle transitions. And if it didn't, or couldn't, there were ways to help. He wasn't afraid.

He'd been present at his mother's death. An extraordinary experience. Over the course of two lifetimes so many of his memories were gone, or hopelessly effaced, but this one was indelible. It would be with him as long as he could think.

Her last days, falling deeper and deeper into unconsciousness. Her last eight hours, on her back, eyes closed, lips parted, breathing rapidly, panting almost. Her last twenty minutes, coughing weakly, unable to clear her throat, unresponsive. He'd taken her hand, then leaned forward and kissed her on the forehead.

Her breathing became more ragged and spasmodic. They called it the rattle of death. Her body shuddered, then convulsed.

Without warning she bolted upright. Her eyes opened wide. Wider than he'd ever seen them, than they'd ever been. They seemed about to pop out of her head. She had beautiful dark eyes, but all he could see, or remember, were the whites. Huge and shiny.

Eerie. Spooky.

His mother.

He tried talking to her. He might as well have been talking to a bench. He planted his face in front of her face, and tried again.

Slowly, she turned her head toward the window, where day had broken and light was spilling in. She held that position rigidly, raptly, as though unable, or unwilling, to tear herself away. Her eyes remained impossibly big and white; her face, preternaturally calm.

He held his breath. Time ground to a halt. One minute, two, forever, until finally she turned away from the window, lay back down, and died.

Ever since that day, he'd wanted to know what she had seen, if anything, or felt, for surely there was something. He wanted to experience it himself, at least improve the odds, but he didn't know how.

His death would be what it was. It would be his. He assumed there was a final common path for everyone, but before that path, a thousand different paths, predetermined, possibly by genetics, possibly behavior—nature, nurture—in death as in life. He'd get what he got.

He'd welcome an epiphany, but wouldn't quarrel with a slower, more gradual demise.

The Ooi was a bump in the road. He'd done everything he could to get it to react, to elicit a response, and still it held out. Alive or not, it was a riddle that begged to be understood.

He loved looking at it. Loved musing about it, which was tantamount to musing about life, what it was and wasn't, what it could be, what was necessary, what wasn't.

Energy, for example: necessary. How else was it able to cling to the rock? What was the source? How was the energy maintained? How was it distributed? Did the Ooi have a hibernation mode? Was that what they were seeing? Were there other stages to its life cycle? Was this an adult? A larva? A seed perhaps? An egg, or mat of eggs, embedded in a matrix? Was its surface a protective casing? A skin of some sort? A shell? And what kind of shell resisted every attempt to see past it?

The longer he sat and observed, the greater his sense there was something there. He felt a connection. What could be more real than that? It seemed plausible, even likely, that he himself was being observed. Which not only answered the question of life, but the far more exciting one of sentience.

He couldn't wait for Dash to arrive. Hated the thought of harming the Ooi, would do everything in his power to limit the damage, but had to know more.

He undid the strap and made his way to the door. He was about to leave when he felt something, a pulse or vibration of some kind, or a sound just beyond the threshold of hearing, something new, previously absent or unexpressed, now suddenly present.

He whirled around.

The Ooi looked different, deeper colored, more saturated, the yellow more lemony, the green more like moss, as though it were concentrating energy, manipulating light somehow. He placed his hand above it, feeling for a change in temperature. Closed his eyes and concentrated. Heard the pounding of his blood, felt it in his fingertips.

Heat?

Yes. A definite feeling of warmth.

Dare he touch it? Actually lay his hand on its surface? Go that far? Take the risk? What was this warmth if not an invitation? Who would fault him?

The answer: he would fault himself if he didn't.

• • •

Three mods and a light year away, while he was making a new friend, Gunjita was working up a sweat. Quads, hams, glutes, fast and slow twitch. It felt good to sweat, like a fire felt to burn. Was it true young people sweated more freely? Seemed true. The glands just seemed to love milking themselves. What better way to spread your already heightened scent, let it do what it was meant to? First dissolve it in liquid, then let it vaporize, like perfume. Fill the air with it. Widest possible coverage and range.

Anyway, it felt good. The perfect balance to her brain, which was doing its own fast twitch. Darting around. Spinning like the cycle. Pondering the mysteries, but at speed.

The thing about alarms, they were happening all the time. All were good, in the sense that being alert and aware were good. Being hyperalert was good, too, it had its place, unless it went on too long, in which case it caused problems. Nervousness, for instance. Anxiety. Paranoia.

You wouldn't want the very alarm you were using to save a life to trigger a mental breakdown. There were enough of those already. The alarm she needed had to walk a thin line.

Again, she found herself thinking that it should be a sexual scent. Sharp and arousing, to the point of dead in the tracks. No prolonged hemming and hawing allowed. No mooning around. The whole purpose, a call to immediate action. Decisiveness.

Pleasure first, then displeasure, right on its heels. The scent would do a hundred and eighty. Sweet would turn to stink: a puzzling, troubling development, and a surefire motivator.

She could start with her own scent. Plenty to work with. Currently, droplets of sweat surrounded her, like effervescent bubbles of champagne. The smell of sweat was not precisely the smell of sex, but it was close. She could distill it, purify it, then modify it. Make it into something irresistible, something you couldn't ignore, you couldn't get enough of, which would mean customizing it person by person, challenging but not impossible. Her scent would be the platform for a limitless number of other scents. Offer these to anyone over the age of sixty. Fifty.

Her gift to the elderly of the planet. A potential project, and a lifesaver to boot. Unfortunately, it wouldn't help Cav: one, because it didn't exist; and two, because he wouldn't take it if it did, for a number of reasons. The most annoying of these at the moment: he was even more intractable than usual. He had crossed, or was about to cross, a line.

His conviction that the Ooi was alive: pure insanity, in her humble opinion. With the slim possibility that it wasn't, that the world (the Ooi, in this case) was as he described, that it existed solely from his perspective, his and his alone, the way insanity worked.

She felt a growing distance from him. A chill in the air when they were together. Her respect for him, a pillar of their relationship, was beginning to erode. Every so often she felt physically repelled by him, which was new, and which she hated.

She carried a double burden of wanting to help and being unable to, or not allowed, and of being stuck with him and unable to get away. Love and loyalty vied with mounting frustration. The balance was not a happy one, nor was it sustainable. She needed a new balance, but something had to give first.

She could leave. Pack her things (there weren't that many), hop the shuttle, and pop down to Earth (where else?). Take some time off. Size things up from a distance. Let him and Dashaud do whatever they were going to. Create some space for herself.

She had a whole new life ahead. Didn't happen every day. What to do with it? Research had been good to her, so probably that. But there was so much she hadn't tried. So much else.

She pedaled faster just thinking about all the possibilities. Didn't notice Cav at first. He kind of snuck up on her.

"I'll come back," he said.

"Ten minutes."

He gave her twenty.

"What's up?" she asked, wiping herself down.

"No response to loud noise. To vibration. To bright light, strobe light. Any light. To touch."

"You touched it?"

"With a glove."

"How did it feel?"

"Firm. Smooth. Maybe a little slippery."

"Cold or hot?" she asked.

"Warm."

"Like what? Room temperature?"

"Warmer."

She needed better than that. "How much?"

"Not much. A little. I didn't have a thermometer."

"And it didn't move, either during or after?"

"No."

"Or before. It's never moved, Cav."

"Not that we've detected."

"Let me guess. You think it's biding its time. Waiting for the right moment. Dormant. Transitional. In stasis."

"Living things move, Gunjita. Maybe it's moving too fast, or too slow, for our eyes and our instruments. Maybe to it, we're immobile. Maybe even undetectable. The burden's on us to find a way to communicate."

"This is crazy, Cav."

"In what way?"

"You're making things up."

"If I had the answers, I wouldn't have to. But I'm ignorant. It could be biding its time. It could be a seed, waiting for the right soil, or substrate, or conditions, to germinate. It could be anything."

"Have you talked to it?" she asked.

"That's funny."

"Have you?"

He averted his face.

"Great," she said.

"Not aloud."

"Wonderful."

He was skating on thin ice. Now would be the time to make light of himself. "Maybe I should try."

She cut him a look.

"I'm joking," he said.

She wasn't in the mood. "Has it talked to you?"

He tried out various answers—truths, half-truths, out-right lies. A change of subject seemed advisable.

"How old do you think it is?" he asked.

"A trillion years."

"Seriously."

"Two trillion."

"From another universe then." It boggled the mind.

"Obviously."

"Ancient." He felt overwhelmed. "Or not. Maybe it's a child where it came from. An innocent."

She was at a loss for words. Didn't know whether to humor him, pity him, or harden her heart.

"You should have asked," she said. "We should have discussed it first."

There was no mistaking what this was about. "There was a window of opportunity. I jumped on it."

"I'm not talking about the HUBIES."

"Dashaud had a window, too."

"Bullshit."

"He's been enhanced. His sense of touch. He can feel anything. Everything."

"Good for him."

"It's been fifty years, Gunjita."

"Sixty."

"He's not the same. Give him a chance."

"Maybe I will. Not up to you."

"You still bear a grudge."

"I don't."

"Then why the fuss?"

She gritted her teeth. "Are you dense?"

He sighed. "I'm sorry. You're right. I should have talked to you first."

"Why didn't you?"

"What would you have said?"

"I have no idea."

"You would have said no."

She tossed this aside. "Moot point. But probably."

No was not an option.

She got off the bike, but he didn't move, effectively blocking her way.

"Was there something else?" she asked. "Because I have work to do."

"Would you do it again?"

"Do what?"

"If you could. Would you juve?"

"Would I juve?"

"Hypothetically."

"A third time? Like Laura Gleem?"

"Hypothetically."

The CEO was etched in her mind. Her image was obviously manufactured. Was there even such a thing as

Laura anymore, beyond the corporate label?

"She hasn't been seen in public since. I'm guessing she's dead."

He didn't care about Laura Gleem. "If there weren't a risk. If it were safe."

"It's not."

"If it were. Proven. Would you do it?"

"A third time?"

"Yes."

The holy grail. That's what they'd called one, then two.

"In a minute," she said.

"You would."

"Yes. In a minute."

"And after that? Would you do it again?"

"A fourth time? I'd be what? Two hundred and fifty years old? Maybe. Or maybe I'd stop. Two hundred and fifty is a lot of years. Maybe enough."

"Why?" he asked. "Why ever stop? You could be immortal."

"Methuselan maybe. Immortal I doubt." She gave him a look. "Is that what this is about? You're morally opposed? It offends your sense of, what? Dignity? Decency?"

"Normalcy."

"It *is* normal. Normal, everyday people do it."

"Not everyone."

"Everyone who can. Or nearly everyone."

"Everyone can't."

"The world isn't fair. Progress is uneven. This isn't news."

"It's numbing," he said. "Living so long. When time is cheap, where's the incentive to make the most of it?"

"The incentive's built in. You need motivation? A deadline? A prod? Since when?"

She pushed past him. Dripping with sweat. Hair plastered to her head. Sleek, redolent, and resolute. An advertisement.

–SIX–

A boy is ripe at every age. A man is ripe until he
becomes over-ripe. He should be eaten before
that date. Afterwards, the best that can be done
is to have him dried and preserved.*

They watched the screen in silence.

"If he crashes, it's on him," she said.

"The shuttle's on autopilot."

"He might decide to disable it. He's just the type."

"Give it a rest," said Cav.

More silence. The shuttle glinted sunlight and steadily
grew in size.

"So he juved."

Cav nodded.

"A bit on the early side, wasn't it?"

---

* From *The Western Fruit-Growers' Association Handbook*, chapter 7,
"Preventing Spoilage."

"Didn't want to wait."

"That I get." Ruby, his mother, had juved at the age of seventy both times. Early for some, not for her. Her health demanded it.

"Go easy on him," Cav pleaded.

"I intend to be very nice. After all, he's my husband's guest. In this, our very own house. Our hideaway. Our nest."

"Very good," said Cav. "Very droll."

"I haven't forgiven you."

He hadn't expected her to. He hadn't quite forgiven himself.

"Maybe with time," he said. "Meanwhile, twist the knife all you like."

"Oh, boo-hoo. Mr. Melodramatic." She punched him on the shoulder. "Get a grip on yourself. Your best friend's about to show up."

Sage advice. He didn't have to be told twice.

"My best friend's been enhanced."

"You said. How's he look?"

"He looks good."

"Different?"

"Younger."

Obviously. "Happy?"

"Sure."

"Eager?"

"Raring to go." This was Dash in a nutshell.

"No change there."

"That's right. Not there."

"Handsome, I assume."

"They're all handsome at that age."

"You know what I mean."

He did. It went without saying. Dashaud Mikelson. A unique and uniquely striking man. "I was handsome once, so I've been told."

"I never noticed."

"You loved me for my brain."

"The same way you loved me."

An old joke.

The ice was melting. He could feel it. Had never wanted anything more.

He hated the thought of pushing her away. Hated the idea of losing her love. This thaw—implicit, unspoken—filled him with hope. He felt himself falling for her just as he had the very first time. And repeatedly since then. Felt the world disappear, his heart expand.

"I love you, Gunjita."

She smiled, without taking her eyes from the screen. "Love you, too, baby."

He felt a stirring. A rare occurrence. Not to be lightly dismissed, or squandered.

He pressed against her hip. Slid his arm around her

neck. Then under her shirt.

"Not now," she said.

"We have time."

She didn't argue. Let him have his way, but eventually lifted his hand from her breast, pressed it to her lips, then returned it to him. "Later, okay?"

She had other things on her mind. He understood this. He had other things on his, too. Things that he'd set in motion. When those things took on a life of their own, there were bound to be disappointments. People couldn't help but get their feelings hurt.

He kissed the top of her head. Their future was approaching. He watched the screen with her, but after a while got tired of it, kissed her again, then left to take a nap.

. . .

Three hours later he was shaking Dash's hand. Then hugging him, which was like hugging a god. They separated, and Dash faced Gunjita.

"Hello," he said.

"Hello, Dashaud."

"Long time."

"Ages."

"It's good to see you."

"Good to see you." He had a smile that lit the room.

That part of him hadn't changed.

"How was your flight?" she asked.

"Uneventful."

Tiptoeing around, and why not?

"First time?"

"In space? No."

"Dash did an internship," said Cav.

"I didn't know."

"Muscle research," said Dash. "Low-grav effects. Early stuff. I was up for a month."

"Before my time."

"It was in my résumé."

"Must have slipped my mind. Can't imagine why."

Dash let it slide. "Cav says you're working on it now."

"Muscles? We're not."

"Actomyosin," said Cav.

"Not by design. But it's there. Can't get away from it."

Dash nodded. "That's how it was with us."

"Pain in the ass getting our cells to divide. Getting consistent motion of any kind."

"Weak signal," he commiserated.

"Creature of Earth. Or was. Now it doesn't know what it's supposed to do. How to behave. A very confused molecule."

"I'd be confused, too," said Dash. "Torn from my momma."

A harmless comment. Sweet even. She wondered what he meant. Realized how little she knew of him. How little she wanted to know. How determined she was, out of spite alone, to keep him at arm's length.

"I'm its new mother," she said. "I'm teaching it to toe the line."

"She's doing all the hard work," said Cav.

"*All* the lifting."

"Not all."

"It's fine, dear. Everyone needs a vacation." She patted his cheek condescendingly, a public display of marital discord she would later apologize for. She was nervous, and not herself. A forgivable offense, given the circumstances.

"Cav says you've been enhanced."

"It's true," said Dash.

"Your sense of touch."

"True again."

"Everywhere?"

"My fingertips mostly."

"Where else?"

A moment's hesitation, as if unsure what she was asking. "Mostly them."

Now she had made him nervous, too. She felt both better and worse. Stifled the urge to ask for an on-the-spot demonstration. But didn't skimp on the feigned enthusiasm.

"Wonderful. Magic fingers. You've come to us in the nick of time. Cav says you can feel everything now."

"Not everything."

"Life? Can you feel that?"

"Yes."

"The difference between life and nonlife?"

"Yes. I believe so."

"Perfect. You can weigh in. Give us your enhanced opinion."

He gave her a look, as if to ask: *Why are you doing this?*

They locked eyes.

"I'll do what I can," he said quietly. "Cav?"

"Yes. By all means. May not have to cut. Wouldn't that be nice?"

"Done any lately?" she asked.

He thought of the fulmar. "A little."

"Still an ace with the knife? You and it still one?"

"I can find my way around."

"Thin slice?"

"Sure. As thin as you need." Puffing out his chest a little.

"What about fixing the specimen? Staining it? Prepping the slide? Can you do that?"

"Not my area of expertise. But I can follow the prompts. How hard can it be?"

"What about reading it?" she asked.

"What is this, a job interview?"

"The job's yours. I'm finding out if you can do it."

"I assume you have software."

"This thing may not be in the database. Probably isn't."

"You're throwing up roadblocks."

"Not me," she said.

"I'm not a pathologist."

Cav had heard enough. "None of us is. But we all know something. Put our heads together, chances are we'll be close to the mark. But first things first. You brought the HUBIES?"

"Brought everything."

"They survived the flight? They're functional?"

"Will be by tomorrow."

"Are they awake?"

"They're warming up."

"I'd like to see." He glanced at Gunjita. "Gunjita's not pleased."

"Don't put words in my mouth. They exist. We might as well use them."

"I agree," he said. "Let them do what they were meant to do. Fulfill their purpose. Assuage our guilt."

"I have no guilt," said Dash. "We were responding to a need."

"Supposed," said Gunjita.

"Idealized," said Cav. "No matter. We took liberties. It's

what we do. Latitude in all things, especially when we wear our research hats. Occupational hazard. Industry standard. You weren't the only one feeding the machine."

"You didn't feel threatened? You weren't afraid?" Dash couldn't believe it. The Hoax was a nightmare that touched every corner or the globe.

Gunjita laughed. "Cav? You're kidding, right? When they filled the skies, and the world was freaking out, he was rubbing his hands, and had a big fat grin on his face. It was a dream come true."

"You exaggerate."

"I was visiting my grandparents," said Dash. "They were scared to death. Everyone was."

"Not everyone."

"It was a lesson," said Cav. "What we will and won't permit. Playing to our greatest fear."

"Annihilation," said Dash.

"Enslavement," said Gunjita.

"Invasion," said Cav. "Ironic, considering what we harbor in our own bodies. How many alien species at last count? How many alien cells? At least half of who we are is nonhuman."

"Your point?" asked Gunjita, who feared a rambling speech.

"We wouldn't be alive were it not for them. They wouldn't be alive were it not for us. We should be more tolerant. We're bigger than we behave. Harmony is woven into our DNA."

"That's very beautiful, Cav," said Dash. "Very eloquent. But you know what they say about harmony."

"What do they say?"

"It's like smoke."

"Who says that?"

"Disharmony does. Second law of thermodynamics. You want it to last, you've got to tighten the screws. Recognize threats. Protect and defend. That's also woven in. Bad things happen when we don't."

"A balance, of course. But how sad if we let ignorance and fear govern us. How counterproductive. We could miss the very things we're looking for. Or could be looking for. Listen to this. Stop me if you've already heard.

"Our retrovirome is what? Eight percent of our genome? Sequences inserted randomly, or nonrandomly, as far back as fifty million years ago. A group has excised it in its entirety, piece by piece, and knitted the pieces together. And guess what? The chain is biologically active. It makes a virus of its own. Brand new, never before seen."

"I don't believe it," said Gunjita. "What's this virus do?"

"It reproduces."

"That's it?"

"They're being very cautious. Very careful."

"No doubt. Mice?"

He nodded.

"And?"

"The sample size is extremely small."

"You're stalling. What's it do?" she asked.

"Hair on the tongue."

"Say again?"

"Little tufts. Presumably because mice have little tongues."

"Human hair?"

He hesitated. "Baboon."

She was less than impressed. "You know these people?"

"I know the journal."

"What's it called?"

It had a long name, sprinkled with the words "Proceedings," "Archive," "Academy," and "Experimental."

"Never heard of it," she said, who had heard of everything.

"Radical stuff," said Cav.

She gave him a look. "Hair on the tongue? You think so? Maybe you want to join forces with them. Work on this radical project. Help them out. No. Wait. I'm sorry. We have our own work. How silly of me. You have a job to do here."

"She means Gleem," said Cav. "They're expecting a miracle."

"They've been more than generous. They deserve one."

"What they're doing is a crime. What they deserve is our contempt."

"Really? In what sense is it a crime?" She hated him when he was like this. Sanctimonious. Naive.

"H82W8 is unnecessary. A waste of resources. In that sense. It's redundant. Reiterative. What good will it do, and for whom?"

"Not for us to decide. Not as long as they're paying the bills."

"How is it redundant?" asked Dash. "You juved."

"Once."

"One time or a hundred. The principle's the same."

"I disagree."

"Are you sorry? Do you regret it?"

"No. Not at all. I don't."

"Neither do I," said Dash. "Some things are overrated. I think we'd all agree. Being young isn't one of them. Look at me. What do you see? A black Viking god, I know. Apart from that."

"What could we possibly see apart from that?" asked Gunjita, all innocence.

"My apologies. I'm blindingly bright, it's true. Cover

your eyes if you have to. Not you, Cav. Look at me. Look at Gunjita."

"I know what youth looks like," said Cav.

"Do you remember how it feels?"

"How can I forget, with the two of you to remind me? It's a beautiful thing. Truly. I couldn't be happier for you."

"Then do it. Juve. What's stopping you?"

Cav heaved a sigh. He had no ready reply. All he could think of was them—Gunjita, Dashaud—and the worry he was causing.

"I hate the thought of losing you," he said. "I love you both so much."

This stopped them in their tracks. Neither of them knew what to say.

Cav welcomed the silence. Then it got to be too much, their speechlessness and abashed, imploding faces yet another responsibility.

He had to distance himself. "You look different," he told Dash.

Gunjita refused to be sidetracked. "You don't have to."

"You don't," said Dash.

"Paler. You look paler. Are you ill?"

"Not ill. Lighter-skinned. Just a shade or two."

Gunjita had noticed at once. She shifted her attention. "Deliberately?"

"No. Why would I do that?"

Inevitably, she thought of his mother. No one prouder of her heritage than Ruby Kincaid, nor as outspoken against racism, which still festered in pockets around the globe, like untreated sewage. Not nearly as bad as it had been. The Hoax, ironically, had united people like never before.

But "not as bad" was not good enough, not by a long shot, not for people like Ruby Kincaid, a tolerant woman except when it came to bigotry and prejudice. Who could be tolerant, much less safe, when certain of humanity's citizens *"remained at war with themselves, drunk on some cockeyed, manufactured pecking order, clucking around like crazy chickens, lacking the decency to keep their mouths shut, and barring that, the common courtesy to have their heads cut off?"*†

"The enhancement," said Cav.

Dash nodded.

"Interfered with melaninization."

Another nod. "More Meissner's, Merkel's, and Pacin-

---

† From one of Ruby's, aka Kleptomania's, performances, for which she dressed as a white Leghorn hen. Gunjita was in the audience. She had been invited by her colleague and friend, Bjorn Mickelson, who was dating Ruby at the time. For Gunjita, it was love at first sight. The spectacle of a beaked and feathered grown woman strutting around and mouthing off had her rolling in the aisle. An eye-popping, mind-blowing, life-altering experience.

ian's, less melanocytes. Crowded them out."

"You took a risk," said Cav.

"What are you talking about?" asked Gunjita.

Five minutes later, after a spirited lesson that began with mechanoreceptors—pressure and motion detectors—in the skin, and ended with one of them, the Meissner corpuscle, named for its discoverer, an accomplished researcher and illustrator, who studied electric fish, developed a technique to preserve organs for years without putrefaction (thereby advancing by leaps and bounds the science of antisepsis), and loved music, Dash returned to Cav's comment about risk.

"A thousand to one."

"Nonetheless," Cav replied haughtily.

Dash was having none of it. "There's a risk anytime you do anything. That includes doing nothing."

"Words of wisdom," said Gunjita. "Are you listening, sweetheart?"

He was, mostly to his own intuition. He sensed a subtle change in Dash, a shyness, a whisper of unhappiness and insecurity.

"Are you pleased with the outcome?" he asked, hoping the answer was yes.

Dash responded by studying his hand, front and back. He'd been so preoccupied with the change in sensation he hadn't spent much time thinking about anything else.

He was blessed with good looks and a strong sense of self. Too handsome by half. Mindful and proud of his roots. All this before juving. Now he looked like he'd been rinsed in skim milk.

A mild shock, like waking from a deep sleep. He felt exposed, defensive.

"I am," he told Cav, puffing out his chest. "Completely satisfied. One hundred percent."

"Then I'm glad. I have a question. Please don't think me rude. You know me better than that."

Dash did, and had no reservations about anything Cav might ask. Happy, even eager, to bare his soul.

Didn't feel quite the same with Gunjita present.

His fingertips had started to throb, as though to remind him that his heart was beating rather hard and fast. At the same time the throb felt independent of his heart, his fingertips an entirely separate organ, restless, hungry for further stimulation and experience, desperate to touch something.

He glanced at Gunjita. Sensibly, kept his hands to himself, though not without an effort.

Focused on Cav. "Ninety percent," he said, coming clean and braving embarrassment.

Cav, who had suspected as much, merely nodded. "My question is this: can you feel the difference?"

"What difference is that?"

"In color. Tint. Shade. Before and after."

Leave it to Cav.

Who proceeded to elaborate. "Our visitor . . . sometimes it looks yellowish-green, sometimes greenish-yellow. I want to know how it's doing that. *If* it's doing that, if it's truly changing."

Whether he could or couldn't differentiate wavelengths of light with his new biology had never entered Dash's mind. Now, of course, he was curious.

He raised two fingers, and gently touched his cheek. Was halted by the bristle, which felt like a bed of nails. Pressed past it, onto his skin itself, which was warm, feathery, and giving. Pillow-soft, barely any resistance, as though it were backing away from his touch, receding. Was it lighter colored than before? Nothing to compare it to. But he felt something.

Amazing.

Also possible: he was making it up. Not his sense of touch at all, but his imagination.

How to distinguish between the two? Gunjita would run an experiment. Cav might run one, too, though just as likely take what he said at face value.

Nothing quite as good as working with Cav.

Who was watching him now. Thinking of the Ooi. Hoping for good news. "Yes? No?"

"Maybe."

"Maybe?"

"Yes. Maybe."

"Weak or solid?"

"Not weak."

"Then solid."

"Yes. Solid. Definitely. A solid maybe."

Cav did not conceal his joy. He took Dash by the arm. "Maybe's good enough for now. Come this way, you beautiful man. Let's put your new talent to work."

–SEVEN–

How do we know a thing? The age-old question.
How to arrive at a mutual, shared understanding? Belief and conviction come too easily to
some; to others, they're as hard to induce as
laughter from a stump.*

Face-to-face with it, Dash thought that Cav was pulling
his leg. That he'd gotten him up under false pretenses, for
a different, as-yet-unannounced purpose.

"You're saying that's alive?"

"Working hypothesis."

"Is it even organic?"

"Best guess: yes."

"It looks like puke."

---

* From *Who and What Can Hurt Us: Rebuttal to Arguments against HU-BIE Research,* by 1URTH Press.

STYLES: loosen

"So I've been told."

They were suited, helmeted, and gloved. Cav extended a hand and draped it lightly atop the Ooi, as he had done previously. All living things on Earth had a pulse of some kind. It varied enormously, and in the long, fruitful history of describing and categorizing life on Earth had often been missed, and a living thing had been taken for nonliving, or possibly once living, now dead. Human perception was limited. Human imagination was also limited: perceptions went unrecognized simply because they had nowhere to go. Add to this the hugeness of the universe, where a creature might exist without a pulse, or with a pulse that beat once every million years. You just never knew.

"You try," he said, removing his hand.

Dash started with a finger, then two, then all five. He felt more glove than anything at first, and pressed slightly harder. Suddenly the Ooi sprang to life with contour and dimensionality: he felt peaks, valleys, ridges, draws, craters. He felt hardness, too, and roughness in spots, smoothness in other spots. All very rocklike. No softness, no give, no inner plasticity or suppleness.

He glanced at Cav, gave a shrug.

"Try closing your eyes. Empty your mind of preconceptions."

He did this, stilled his breathing, and alerted himself

to the faintest, weakest signal.

He waited.

And waited.

At length he felt something.

Or almost something. An incipient something, like a secret about to be spoken, a feint followed by a gradual retreat, an impending sneeze, or rather the suggestion of a sneeze, a sneeze that fizzles. Like that. Present for the briefest time, then gone.

"What?" asked Cav. "What is it?"

"It disappeared."

"What disappeared?"

He tried to describe it.

"Movement? A pulse of some kind?"

"Maybe. I don't know. Probably nothing. Probably me, not it. I need to touch it with my bare skin. Without gloves."

"Yes. Me, too. And smell it. And taste it."

Dash gave him a look. "Your tongue? Really?"

"Or yours."

A joke, from anyone else.

"Is it more sensitive, too?"

"My tongue?"

Cav nodded. "To touch."

He hadn't noticed. Taste was such a dominant sense. "Leave it to you to ask."

Cav was thinking about hair on the tongue, baboon or otherwise, and how it might be put to use.

Dash pressed the tip of his against his teeth. "And the risk of contamination?"

"Use a condom."

"On my tongue? Wouldn't that defeat the purpose?"

"We'll leave taste for last. How's that?"

. . .

While the HUBIES were thawing, and the men were manning around, Gunjita was in the cupola, debating with herself. They'd been on the station nearly a month, had less than a week remaining, but she wanted to leave at once.

It wasn't because of Dash. It wasn't the HUBIES. It wasn't Cav's craziness around the Ooi. The craziness was a veil.

It was what was going to happen when the veil came off.

He was planning to end his life. She'd seen the drugs he'd brought and tried to hide. She knew what was going through his mind.

The idea was awful in too many ways to count.

What she didn't understand: if there was anything Cav hated more than deceit, it was self-deceit. Honesty-

Whatever-the-Cost was his nom de guerre. So why was he acting this way? He seemed to be lying to her and to himself. Was he undecided? Did he need more time?

Did it matter? Either way, she was a hostage.

She felt trapped. The tension onboard was like a cage, and she longed to break free of it.

Earth was dark beneath her. Beads and blotches and smears of light glittered the globe. Then sunrise came, and the globe turned blue and white.

Blue for the Indian Ocean, which spooled into view. White for the clouds, which hung like shreds of paper over it. Also over the landmass of southern India, half hiding its parched brown interior, and the fringe of green along the Kerala coast. Sri Lanka, a recent powerhouse in the global economy, appeared to be nosing its way toward the mainland, with the intention of taking a bite.

And now the Himalayas, a long, curved fold in the Earth's pie crust, sprinkled with powdered sugar. The Ganges snaking south. Rishikesh, her birthplace, in the foothills, on the great river's shore.

She thought of her parents, both of them deceased. Her father, a happy, soft-spoken teacher. Her mother, a successful businesswoman, energetic and ambitious. Gunjita took after her mother. Had headed a lab for the better part of two lifetimes. Had shaped and commanded battalions of scientists. Had created a stronghold of research, which had not only withstood the steady assault on science but had become iconic in the field. A safe, protected place. A haven for free but disciplined thinkers. A refuge for the best and the brightest, where failures, by definition, rarely occurred.

She was on leave, could return at any time. Hard to think of anything to rival it, though she could do without the money part. The funding, the begging, the paperwork, the courtship. It was a constant struggle to survive.

But the life of the mind. Of discovery. What could be better? What exercise could come close to the exercise of logic?

She made a fist of her hand. Opened it, closed it. Hardened her abs, and ran her fingers down the ladder.

There wasn't much of one. The runs were soft and ill-defined. She'd never had the inclination or the time to make them otherwise. Now she thought, why not? Nothing wrong with definition. Might be nice for a change.

She could take one of the shuttles and escape. Become a gym rat instead of a lab rat, or in addition. Widen the scope of her life. Embrace the physical. Add muscle strength and flexibility to what she already mentally possessed.

She could be an athlete.

A dancer.

A reforester. A firefighter. Plenty of work on Earth for both of those.

A cop.

A tunneler. The trans-Pac tube was always looking for muscle and brawn.

Her father had practiced yoga. She could do that, but seriously this time.

Her very first memory was yoga-related. A harsh, irritating smell: smoke, she was told later. Her father had let something burn on the stove. Lost in his head, the story went. Or on his head. Salamba Sirsana. So maybe not that pose.

But there was another smell along with the harsh one, perfumey and sweet. It might have occurred later, or possibly at the same time. The two were interwoven in her mind, indelibly linked: harshness and sweetness. She never asked herself why. But when she got older, she started asking other questions, like what, where, and how.

What made a smell? How was smell recognized? What did the brain do with it, and how did it decide which smells to funnel where, which to network, and which to disregard? Was there truly such a thing as odorless? A human being had six million smell receptors, compared to a dog's two hundred and twenty mil. Would we be better off with a few more? A few less? Was there really a difference between women and men in smelling ability, and if so, how could this be exploited?

So much to learn. Such a core sensation. So primitive, and resistant to time's corrosive effect.

She would never forget her father's smell. He was the family cook. His fingertips were stained with turmeric and cumin. But stronger than that smell, more deeply ingrained in her, was the scent of his oiled hair, which made her forever partial to roses.

When it came to smell, everybody had a story.

But not everybody cared to unravel the story as much as Gunjita did. She had helped develop the OE vaccine, was at the forefront of OSN transplantation. There'd be no Watchdog Council without her, no ORA. No HUBIES, either.

She'd blamed Dash at first. Then herself, for training and mentoring him. Reasonable targets, but ridiculous. She might as well have blamed the Swiss for Swiss cheese. Or Albert, for the explosion.

He was a scientist, same as her. He took what he learned and ran with it. Not only that, he responded to a call. A loyal citizen of Earth. What better justification?

If only they looked different. Stranger, more alien, less human. If only they didn't resemble young children so much.

How did he wrap his head around that?

She was glad that he'd come, despite herself. Of course it was awkward, but they were adults. They'd get past it.

He was good for Cav, which meant good for her. Maybe he could talk him out of his madness.

She checked the time. The moment of truth was approaching. Mentally, she'd been preparing herself. She was looking forward to doing without her helmet and cumbersome suit. Had to be grateful to them for that. Gratitude was better than much of what she felt. It would be good to put a face on her nightmare at last.

• • •

A HUBIE was far superior to a canary: more sensitive, more reliable, more specific to humans. More humane to canaries, too, or would have been if floater panic hadn't driven canaries to the brink of extinction. With more smell receptors than a dog, more smell genes than an elephant, a HUBIE responded to airborne toxins in one of two ways: swiftly, in the case of toxins originating from nonorganic material; marginally less swiftly in the case of toxins originating from organic material, such as living- or recently living things. Death in minutes as compared to hours, occasionally a full day. A bell-shaped curve.

They'd been functional and in place for nearly a full day.

Cav was champing at the bit.

"Let's do this right," Dash cautioned.

"We're ten minutes shy. I say twenty-three hours, fifty minutes is enough. Help me out here, Gunjita."

"I'm with Dash."

"Dash's being nitpicky."

"Dash's acting like a grown-up. He wouldn't have to, if you weren't being such a child."

"You're despots. Both of you."

"Poor baby. Close your eyes. Take a deep breath. Repeat these words silently to yourself: time is an illusion. Time does not exist."

"Eight," said Dash. "Now less."

. . .

Cav was the first one in. Gunjita followed him, with Dash taking up the rear. The three HUBIES were spaced equidistantly in a triangle around the asteroid and the Ooi, harnessed to the floor to keep them from drifting.

Pop-dolls, some people called them. Raggedy-Anns.

Cav went to each in turn, bowed his head, clasped his hands, and mouthed a prayer. To Gunjita, an empty gesture. To Dash, melodramatic and purposeless. But Cav was Cav.

The HUBIES, naturally, paid no attention. Their eyes protruded from their sockets, and appeared frozen in place: they looked too big for their faces, which looked too big for their heads. Silky brown hair fell over their narrow foreheads and partially hid the awful backward anencephalic slope of their skulls. Their noses were fleshy and free-moving, the nostrils hooded by a short, tubular fold of skin. Their lips were pink as peonies. Their arms dangled lifelessly by their sides. Their legs, also lifeless. They looked, on the whole, like bizarre, inflatable dolls.

Gunjita approached the nearest one. Her heart was hammering in her chest. It didn't appear to notice her at first. A HUBIE had eyes but nowhere to put sight, no visual cortex, and was effectively blind. Had nowhere to put sound, either. But its nose was all-seeing, all-knowing, and was quick to respond.

It swept the air from side to side, sniffing, sampling, as though she were a cone of smell. Rapidly, it honed in on its target, and the tubular cowl of skin retracted to reveal two large, moist, saucer-shaped nostrils that looked like black moss. They quivered with activity. Moments later, the HUBIE's eyes swiveled in unison until they were centered on her face.

It was purely reflexive. A HUBIE was blind. Not that it mattered: she felt transparent.

She'd seen photos, but this was her first face-to-face. Save for the repulsion, the pity and the guilt, it wasn't that bad.

Actually, it *was* that bad.

She gagged, and nearly lost her lunch. It was like being poisoned, seeing it there, staring her in the face.

Noiselessly, Dash materialized beside her. The HUBIE's nose twitched, as it picked up the new scent.

"Well?"

"Well what?"

"How are you doing?"

"How do you think?"

"Shocked?"

"Don't be stupid."

Not a good beginning. The HUBIE was burning a hole in her brain, but then it broke contact, and transferred its blind stare to Dash. She felt as if a weight had been lifted.

"They take some getting used to," he said.

"I doubt that's going to happen. I hope it won't."

She knew it would.

He glanced at her, looking concerned.

After a while she said, "I suppose it was inevitable. Once we started making better humans, we'd make lesser ones."

"They're not really human."

"Human enough."

"They're not unhappy, Gunjita. They're doing what they were meant to do. If anything, they're happy for that. They're certainly not uncomfortable. They don't hurt. They feel no pain."

Longer

She knew the song and dance. Had her own opinion.

"They have brains, don't they?"

"Primitive. Extremely. No cortex. No awareness. If there *is* pain, they don't know it. If they know it, they don't care. It doesn't bother them. They don't suffer."

"So you say."

"It's a fact."

"*We* suffer," she said.

He looked pained. "Do you? Really? Is that true?"

"Humanity suffers."

"But you? Do you?"

"Why? Do you think I shouldn't? I should be made of sterner stuff?"

"I thought you were."

"I am."

"Well then."

"They were ill-conceived. They should never have been made. You could have designed something else. *Anything* else."

He studied the HUBIE, considering this, searching for flaws. Blind, limp, imbecilic. Unable to speak. Unable to hear. Unable to think.

His creation.

He reached up and touched it, laid his hand on its chest, as he would a patient. Felt its lively, cheerful pulse.

"We could have done better," he confessed. "If there's

ever a next time, we will."

"You were pressured, no doubt."

"Yes. Of course. But in the end we called the shots."

"The team."

"Yes."

"You played a significant role?"

Not the time to boast. "I was there."

"Inner circle?"

He nodded, remembering the buzz. The excitement. The camaraderie.

He'd never thanked her. "I wouldn't have been there if it weren't for you."

"A dubious honor."

"You could have hung me out to dry."

"I was doing my job. You deserved to be in a lab. A good one. Tell me something. Their design. Was that aimed at me?"

"At you?"

"Out of spite. For revenge." It felt good to finally get it off her chest. His response barely mattered.

"No," he said. "I didn't have time to be angry. We were too busy. I licked my wounds and moved on."

She remembered things differently. A superficial licking maybe, but no healing. A chill whenever they were in the same room, which happened periodically over the years.

She felt it less now. "You vowed to get back at me."

"Heat of the moment. Shoot from the hip."

"I always wondered."

"You can stop. I would never do something like that."

True or false? Was it even important? People changed.

"They look like children," she said.

"They're tools, Gunjita. Instruments."

"Damaged."

"No. Not damaged. Preventers of damage. Shields. Don't think of them as children, but as soldiers."

"Protecting us."

"Yes."

"Sacrificing themselves."

"If necessary."

She tried to see it. Appreciated different perspectives, theoretically at least.

"They're both," she said.

"If you wish."

"Either way, they're ours. Yours and mine."

"I'm proud of what they are."

"I pity them."

"I'm sorry you feel that way."

He wasn't a bad man. Nothing like that. Better, in fact, than she expected. But better had limited appeal.

"I'm sorry you don't."

. . .

Cav, meanwhile, was bent over the Ooi, sucking in air, breathing audibly through his nose. In and out, in and out, sampling, just as the HUBIES did. Lacking a free-moving noodle, he moved his head side to side, up and down, a technique used by animals and taught to him by Gunjita, the expert. He closed his eyes and willed himself to take everything in.

Recognition could come and go in an instant. Alternately, it could take hours, weeks, years. This was the book on unknown forms of life, and seemed reasonable, though of course no one knew.

What he could say so far: the Ooi had a clean, faintly metallic scent. He sniffed several times in rapid succession, then inhaled deeply, filling his nostrils and lungs. Nearly impossible to distinguish it from the asteroid. Was this purposeful, a kind of camouflage? An adaptation?

Interesting.

He leaned in closer, until he was nearly touching it, breathed on it, moved his head back and forth, giving it the opportunity to smell him.

He was playing with fire, and he knew it. Gunjita thought he was crazy. Dash probably, too. Maybe he was. But maybe not. Plenty of people, if they knew, would have been in his corner, cheering him on. Crazy? Hardly. More like sanity itself. Just tell us when and where. We're with you 100 percent.

Plenty believed it had already happened. A fait accompli. *They* were among us, and had been for years.

Some people said they were very nice.

Others, not so nice.

Some, that sex with one was the very best thing. Some said the worst. One man had reliable information that they had no genitals. He was met by a chorus of jeers: everyone knew they had sex organs everywhere. What was he, a prude?

Cav kept half an ear out for these people. They had their ideas. They weren't scientific ideas. Most were predictably ridiculous. But every so often one would stand out.

A recent favorite: the One Alien Theory, which posited an enormous, invisible, oyster-shaped entity, embracing and nurturing the Earth as it would its own pearl. A sentient bivalve, it was dismayed to see what was happening to its precious creation. Dismayed and angry.

This explained the outbreaks of planetary fear, suspicion, and anxiety that happened now and again. Oysters weren't known to lash out, but neither were they known to be especially forgiving. And this was a big one. No one knew what to expect.

Cav felt the same about the Ooi. No problem so far, but how would it react to being cut?

Which, having run out of options, was up next.

But first, a last chance. Dash had taken off his gloves.

Cav already had his hand on the Ooi, feeling its cool, hard surface. He moved aside, letting Dash take his place.

Dash repeated what he'd done before, resting his fingertips lightly at first, then pressing them down more firmly. Cav and Gunjita watched as the tension slowly built.

It wasn't the sole source of tension. Cav was aware of the strain between him and Gunjita. He was responsible for it, and wished it didn't exist. He would talk to her, try to smooth things out, though he wasn't optimistic.

"I can't be sure," Dash said at last.

"You feel something?"

"Yes and no."

"Which is it?"

"Movement. Maybe. Maybe a vibration. Very faint. It comes and goes. Maybe nothing."

"Color?" asked Cav.

Dash threw up his hands.

"I smell roses," said Gunjita.

She might have screamed "Fire!" at the top of her lungs the way the two of them looked at her.

"For real?" asked Dash.

She rolled her eyes. "It's time to stop fooling around. We need a piece."

Cav nodded, inhaling deeply through his nose. "Maybe it knows. Maybe roses is its SOS. The precatastrophe alarm you've been looking for. Forgive us," he told the Ooi. Then to Dash, "Start with its edge. See if you can peel it back."

They'd brought their instruments. Dash tried the spatulated knife first. Couldn't separate the Ooi from the rock cleanly, in one piece. Looked to Cav for guidance.

Cav told him to proceed.

Using a scalpel this time, and not just any scalpel but one forged in the legendary foundry of Bethlehem, Brokkr & Doome, with a laser spine, an intercalated hypercrystalline edge, and oscillating nano-teeth. A tool preferred by professionals. Dash loved how it felt: alert, alive, like an extension of his own hand. He neatly shaved off the tip of one of the Ooi's arms, continuing the cut into the underlying rock, removing both as a unit.

Cav winced, but bore witness. He was spellbound. The exposed surface did not ooze or bleed.

"Self-healing?" he wondered aloud. An attribute basic to all life. He glanced at Dash, who shook his head.

"Too fast."

"To us," said Cav.

"I've never seen it so rapidly."

"No. Yes. That's what makes it exciting."

"Maybe it's thicker-shelled than we thought."

"It doesn't have a shell," said Gunjita.

"Or it wasn't bothered. The amount you shaved off didn't matter. It was like paring a fingernail."

"I could make a bigger cut."

"No, no. This is enough. More than enough." He cradled the slender, crescent-shaped specimen in his palm, feeling like a guardian of the universe. It was weighty but weightless.

Carefully, he returned it to Dash, who sealed it in a bottle in preparation for microtomal slicing, fixation, and staining. Each a separate procedure, none of which, given Dash's experience, or rather lack thereof, was guaranteed to succeed.

"Wish me luck," he said.

"How about a helping hand?" Gunjita offered.

"Yes. Please. By all means."

Cav felt a stab of jealousy. A stab of sadness. A stab of relief.

"Coming?" she asked.

"No. You go. I'll stay for a while. I'm good."

• • •

Once in the lab, Gunjita took charge. She knew where

everything was, and Dash tried to stay out of her way. It brought back memories.

"Feels like old times," he said.

She wasn't interested in reminiscing. "So what do you think?"

"About Cav?"

"First the Ooi. Truthfully."

"Truthfully? It looks like puke."

"Is it alive? Could it have ever been?"

"Ever?"

"Forget ever. Living or not?"

"Cav thinks so."

"Forget Cav."

"I can't. You shouldn't, either."

"What does that mean?"

"He's the reason I'm here. I couldn't *not* come. He wants to die. The Ooi is keeping him alive."

"You underestimate him, Dash. He's keeping himself alive until he makes up his mind. So far he hasn't decided. Our Ooi is a pretext. A placeholder. A sham."

"Convenient that it arrived when it did."

"Purely coincidence. If it hadn't been this, it would have been something else."

"He wants to live."

"He doesn't know what he wants."

Uncharted territory for Dash. He felt as if he were being forced to watch something he shouldn't have to. He felt paralyzed, hamstrung.

"I don't understand. What's so wrong about living? What's so difficult? Is he sick? Is he hiding something?"

"He feels guilty."

"Cav?" He swallowed a laugh.

"No joke. He's been privileged all his life. That includes the privilege of being open-minded. The privilege of believing in fairness, and justice for all. Now it's caught up with him. He sees the hypocrisy. If everyone can't juve—and everyone can't—then no one should."

"Never going to happen."

"Of course not. But he's doing his part. Making his point. Staking the high ground."

"Martyring himself," said Dash.

"It eases his conscience."

She was angry. And hurt. It helped to talk.

"I sound harsh."

Dash was sympathetic. "He's a handful."

"A handful and a half. I love him very much. I'm proud that he has principles. I'm proud that he doesn't settle for the easy way out, that he stands up for what he believes is right. In a way I'm proud of what he's doing. Or what he's thinking about doing. He makes it hard not to be."

She pulled out jars, canisters, various tools, and instruments, slamming them down on the bench, then compulsively arranging them. Making things neat and tidy was a tic that came out when she was stressed. Work was her love and joy, but also how she dealt with strong emotions. Dash remembered this about her. Like after their crash and burn. How businesslike she became. How completely she shut him out.

He wanted to say something to her now. Do something. Put the past to bed. Be a friend. Comfort her.

He had a strong urge to take her in his arms, give her a warm and reassuring hug, but fortunately the urge was short-circuited by the voice of reason, which stayed his hand. He went with words instead, sidestepping almost certain disaster.

"You have every right to be proud. He's a great man. One of a kind. He sets the bar high, though. Tough living up to his standards."

"He puts himself on a pedestal."

"Interesting," said Dash. "I thought that was me, putting him there. I know I do. Warts and all. He deserves to be there."

"I wish he'd come down." She felt tied in knots. "Now I sound like a hypocrite."

"You don't."

"It's his specialty. Making us doubt and second-guess ourselves."

"It's his gift. We don't have to accept it. I haven't, not

this time. There's no doubt in my mind what he should do."

"He does have a point."

"About what? Unfairness? Inequality? There's less and less every day."

"Less is still too much."

"Any is too much," said Dash. "But the tables are turning. The scales are evening out. It won't be this way forever."

"Won't that be nice? But what about now? What about the world we're building now? People living longer and longer. Overpopulation. Overcrowding. Resources stretched to the limit. Mental and physical stress. There're so many of us. Privilege or no privilege, it's not healthy. Not for us, and not for Momma."

"Cav says this?"

"*I* say this. But yes. Of course. Not only him. It's there for anyone to see."

"We'll find a way," said Dash. "Always have."

"You think so?"

"I do."

"You're optimistic."

"I am. Science and technology are powerful tools. I have faith."

She was feeling wicked. "Here's an idea. How about another invasion? A real one this time. Followed by mass extermination. Lightening the load on . . . well, every-thing."

"Hopefully, we'll find a better solution than that."

"Maybe our Ooi is an advance scout."

He gave her a look. This wasn't the Gunjita he remembered. That Gunjita didn't have a cynical bone in her body. That Gunjita was earnest and sincere. She wouldn't have known sarcasm if it bit her in the face.

This one had an edge.

"You're not serious," he said.

"He has a point is all I'm saying. He could stick around and try to sell it. Work to solve the problem. Instead he comes here and contemplates suicide." She felt at the end of her rope. "I wish our Ooi *were* alive. Cav might juve if it were. No guarantee, but the hook would be that much harder to get out."

"It could be."

"Alive? I don't believe it."

"I felt something."

"I'm sure you did, but what?"

"Movement."

"That no one else can feel."

"I wish you could," he said.

"Your own pulse maybe."

"Possibly."

"The point being—"

He cut her off. "I know the point. It's no proof. Let's do an experiment."

"What kind of experiment?"

"I'll feel your pulse."

"I can do that myself."

"Not just your heartbeat. All your pulses."

She eyed him. "Meaning what?"

"Your ebb and flow. Your waves and vibrations. Your internal flux."

"My flux? No, thanks."

"I'll interpret them," he said, gaining momentum. "You tell me what you've been thinking and feeling, and I'll tell you what I found. We'll see how closely the two match."

"You'll confirm my thoughts and feelings?"

"Scientifically. Not only the ones you're aware of."

"My secrets? My private life? My precious, highly personal, highly confidential flux?" She could barely keep from laughing in his face.

"Everything. You can't believe how sensitive I've become."

"Oh, I believe it."

"Just give it a try."

"Close your mouth," she said. "You're salivating."

He reached for her hand.

"No, you don't."

She refused to give it to him, wanting to be neither

guinea pig, object of desire, nor inspiration for his stale, pale fantasy life. As a come-on, it was lamer than a broken-down horse.

Though she couldn't help being curious. Not to mention, she could use a break from Mr. I-Want-To-Kill-Myself. He was an albatross around her neck. A little fun and games, a little goofiness, would be a breath of fresh air.

"Very lightly," she agreed, extending her wrist.

He held his hand just above her. His expression turned inward and intensified, as though he were entering a new state of mind or consciousness, leaving their world for another. His fingertips seemed to have a life of their own, slowly drifting downward until they brushed her skin.

His touch was gentle and feather light. She felt a tingle, which was nice, though nothing like the electric shock she'd once experienced. And it didn't last.

A short time later, she ended the experiment, pulling her hand back, breaking contact.

"So?" she asked. "Pick the lock? Crack the safe? Find what you were looking for?"

"Blew the door right off."

"Ouch. Explosive."

"Let's compare notes. What are you thinking and feeling?"

"You tell me."

There were a number of things he wanted to say. Almost all were in the realm of guesses, hopes, and dreams. He knew enough to tread lightly.

"I think you're interested."

"In you?"

"Yes."

"That's what *you're* thinking."

"You're not?"

"Among many other things. *Many* other."

"So yes."

Was he kidding? "It's not going to happen, Dash. So drop it."

"What's not? I don't know what you mean."

"I'm not going to sleep with you."

"*Sleep* with me?" He looked shocked.

She didn't buy it. "Let's change the subject. How's your mother?"

"*Sleep* with you?"

"Your mother, Dash. How's she doing?"

"That's not what I was thinking."

"Has she seen you lately?" Not, *have you seen her?*

"She's old."

"But not blind. What was her reaction?"

"Ask her."

"Don't pout."

"Don't presume," he shot back.

She and Ruby hadn't spoken in nearly sixty years. Unlikely that was going to change. Juving was a miracle, but to friends and families it created havoc. Or it could. Parents younger than their kids, and acting like kids. Grownups transformed into twenty-year-olds with something to prove. Taboos questioned. Traditions turned on their heads.

Ruby had not taken kindly to Gunjita sleeping with her son. Gunjita had not taken kindly to it herself, once she came to her senses.

Professionally, the fallout was severe. Sleeping with a student was wrong in so many ways. Changing mores had not changed this essential fact. Not yet. Dash hadn't made things any easier for her. She nearly lost her lab, not to mention her career.

Eventually, she recovered. The incident receded into the past. She got back on her feet. Professionally, it was pretty much smooth sailing after that. Personally, there was no point in continuing to beat herself up.

Ruby, unfortunately, didn't share that opinion. There was one particularly ugly shouting match, at a restaurant no less. Ruby did the shouting. Frozen to her chair, Gunjita sat and listened, mouth agape, then excused herself from the table. She went to the restroom, took a number of deep breaths, then left. Walked right out of the restaurant, and kept walking. Hadn't laid eyes on Ruby since.

"She can't have been happy."

"She's my mother," said Dash, as though no further explanation were needed. He picked up a small, stainless-steel tray, studying his reflection in it.

"There's a black that eats lasers," he said. "You know the one I'm talking about? Absorbs all light."

"I've heard of it."

"They've invented something even blacker. Blackest black ever. A black hole black."

Gunjita recalled Ruby's search for something like that. "Grabs your attention, I'm guessing."

"Swallows it. If she could, she'd be that. She painted herself once for a performance. Freaked people out."

"Kleptomania had a reputation for that."

He nodded. "The Stealer of Hearts and Souls. The Robber of Self-Righteousness."

"The Thief of Hypocrisy," she added.

"All that. Happiest day of her life."

"Is she still performing?"

"She killed herself."

Gunjita was stunned. "Who did? You said . . . Oh my god!"

He heaved a sigh, drawing the moment out, being something of a performer himself. The bearer of post-surgical good or bad news more times than he could count. He knew what suspense could do, and on principle avoided it.

But this was payback.

Gunjita was reeling. "Your mother killed herself? You said she was fine. I can't believe it."

He let her hang a bit longer before coming clean.

"She retired. Onstage. A kite, a knish, and a good-bye kiss. Her final bow. You didn't hear?"

Her relief was immediate and immense. She slumped like a rag, then picked herself up, and shoved him in the chest.

They flew apart. Several pieces of lab equipment flew with them. Gunjita couldn't have cared less.

"You know something, Dash?"

"What's that?"

"You're an asshole."

At last, a little warmth. A little affection.

"And you do want to sleep with me. It's the truth. You shouldn't protest. I don't mind that you do. But I'm curious. Is it coming from you? Or did Cav put you up to it?"

–EIGHT–

When you live a long life, there are things you forget. Some you choose to forget. Some, simply, are forgettable. This is natural.

When you live three long lives, with three times the experiences in a one lifetime–sized brain, the forgotten begins to pile up. By the end the pressure can be immense, rather like a storm about to break. A neurobarometrically volatile time in one's life. You may hear voices. You may be jittery and restless. Wake frequently at night. You may feel out of sorts, as if you're not yourself. Don't be alarmed.

Alternatively, you may feel more yourself than ever. Don't be alarmed by this, either.*

---

* From the manual: *Choosing Long Life: What to Expect,* chapter 11, "The Final Days."

Gunjita was asleep. Cav slid into the mod, trying not to disturb her.

She opened her eyes.

"Sorry," he said.

"It's okay. I'm awake."

"You know a guy named Cantrell?"

"No. Should I?"

"I just got off the comm with him. He heard about our Ooi. Had some questions."

"He's a reporter?"

"An interested party. His words. A friend of Dash. Also his words." He told her what he knew about him.

"What does Dash say?"

"That he's clever. Smart. A bit of an oddball."

"How'd he get past security?"

"One of his talents, I take it."

"What did you tell him?"

Cav loosened his belt and started to undress. "We're half-alien to begin with. Xenophobia is oxymoronic."

"Is that what you said?"

"I'm saying it to you."

She'd heard it a hundred times before. "Did you tell him it was alive?"

"No."

"Dead?"

He got his pants as far as his ankles, but couldn't free

his legs. "When did we develop such an antagonism to other species?"

"Did you say 'species'? Did you use that word?"

"I might have. I don't remember."

It was only a species if he said so publicly. From that point on, right or wrong, they would have no peace. The world would have no peace. The Hoax had proven this. Not a restful time for planet Earth.

And the instigator? The provocateur?

He'd be a hero to all the wrong people, a laughingstock to everyone else.

At present his pants were stuck. He couldn't get them off, and was thrashing back and forth like a fish on a hook. He was a laughingstock now.

She chided herself for the thought.

"When they tried to kill us," she said. "Or killed us, without trying. Let's see. When did that start? How about the beginning of time."

"Most of them don't. Nature preaches harmony, mostly."

"*We* preach harmony. Nature preaches tooth and claw."

"When did you get so cynical, Gunji?"

"When did you get so soft?"

He felt the opposite. Courageous. Defiant. Scared, sure, but you couldn't be courageous if you weren't.

"I have something to tell you," he said.

"So tell me."

"I love you very much."

"You have a strange way of showing it."

"I'm sorry. I know. What I've put you through the last few weeks . . . I can't imagine what it's been like. In return, you've shown me nothing but patience and kindness. You've been incredible."

"Thank you, Cav."

"You *are* incredible."

She kissed him, then took hold of his pants and yanked.

"Nicely done," he said.

She turned off the light.

"Have you given any more thought to your precatastrophe alarm?" he asked.

"A little. Not much. Why?"

"It's a good idea."

"Maybe. We'll see."

"If not that, then what? What next?"

"Not sure. I have some ideas."

"Care to share them?"

She tossed a few out, wondering where this sudden curiosity was coming from.

"Will you teach?"

"I don't know."

"You should. You're a wonderful teacher. Passionate.

Inspiring. I remember the first time I heard you. The lecture you gave. I haven't been the same since."

"That's nice," she said. "I might. I might try something else. I haven't decided."

"Doesn't matter."

She rolled on her side, and faced his dark bulk. "How doesn't it matter?"

"You'll be good at whatever you do."

"How do you know that?"

"Not only good, but happy. You'll be happy. I know because I know you."

"I hope I will be. I plan to be."

"I love you, darling."

She felt a growing uneasiness: so much affection and encouragement, welcome at any other time, only half-welcome now because of the feeling that something was off.

She rolled onto her back, and closed her eyes. "We have a busy day tomorrow. Time to sleep. Good night, Cav."

"Good night, sweetheart."

. . .

The next time she opened her eyes, it was morning, and he was gone. She dressed, and went looking for him, checking the bay first. The HUBIES floated like hot-air balloons. It sickened her to look at them. The Ooi was yellow-green, and save for the small missing part, unchanged.

She found him with Dash in the lab, the two of them scrolling through a series of images that looked like smears of paint.

Dash looked up when she arrived. His eyes were bloodshot. His voice, tired and contrite.

"It didn't work. Not sure why. Maybe how I mixed the stain. Or something in the transfer."

"You said you could do it."

"I said I'd try."

"The slide is worthless?"

He stood aside and motioned to the images. "See for yourself."

She ran through them rapidly. There were slashes, drips, and splotches of stain, some of them translucent, some opaque. Nothing close to informative.

"A waste," she said.

"Maybe not," said Cav. "Maybe it's telling us something. There's a message here."

She ignored him. "You're going to make another one?"

"I can. No guarantee."

"Make three," she said. "Let's learn from our mistake."

"It's unnecessary," said Cav.

"No you don't. It *is* necessary."

"It's not." He cleared his throat. "I have something to say."

It sounded serious. She wished she were elsewhere. "I have something to say first. We're done with the HUBIES. They've served their purpose. We have no further use for them. We should put them to sleep."

Cav raised his eyebrows.

Dash looked like he'd been dropped from a cliff.

"We should put them out of their misery," she added.

"They're not in misery," Dash reminded her.

"They've done what they were asked to do."

"Made to do," he said.

"Precisely. Cav?"

He opened his mouth to answer, but no words came out. In their place he felt a flutter in his chest, as if a moth were trapped. His vision blurred. The room receded. He couldn't feel his legs.

Abruptly, the flutter stopped.

Gunjita was staring at him.

He gathered himself. "A mercy killing."

"You could call it that," she said.

"I believe in mercy."

"We all believe in mercy," said Dash, not to be left out.

"Then we're agreed."

Cav frowned. "But I don't agree. I'm sorry, but I don't.

We don't know what mercy is in this case. What it is to them. We're ignorant. To them it might be the opposite of what we think. How can we put them to sleep? We can't."

"We *made* them," Gunjita retorted.

The words seemed to reverberate with self-recrimination. Neither man spoke. Moments later, when she realized what had just come out of her mouth, she rushed to explain herself.

"What I meant . . . We're responsible. Without knowing what they want, we have to guess. Put ourselves in their shoes. Ask ourselves what we would want."

Cav felt that she was talking about him. He was filled with love for her, filled with pride to be her husband, filled with admiration. But he could only say what *he* would want, not what they would, and what he wanted was the freedom to choose.

"We *could* guess," he said gently. "I wish I could say we should. But I don't believe it. We have no right to dictate their fate. When and how they live and die is not our business. Our business is us.

"Which leads me to what I want to say. It might ease the sting. I'm giving up the fight. No more arguing about our Ooi. No more pushing down your throats a pill that obviously doesn't agree with you. There's a time for talk and a time for silence."

"Hallelujah," she said.

"You're changing your opinion?"

"Give an inch, they ask for a mile." Cav shook his head, and smiled. "I'm not objecting to yours. Say whatever you like. I won't contest or contradict anything you report."

"What's the catch?" asked Gunjita.

"No catch."

She didn't believe it. "Hear that?" she told Dash. "That ringing in your ears? That hole in the air? That vacuum? That's the sound of a shoe not dropping." She locked eyes with her husband. "Stop being such a pussy."

She was right. In addition to being his soul mate, she was his weather vane. In addition to that, his rock and his pillar. He needed her, now more than ever. He needed every bit of strength he could muster.

"I have a favor to ask."

Here it comes, she thought.

"I want to be alone."

Dash nodded. It seemed a reasonable request.

"Alone alone," he added.

Another nod from Dash. "Sure. Why not?"

"You don't get it," said Gunjita. "He wants us out of here. Gone."

"Is that right, Cav?"

"He's had enough of us. He's giving us the boot."

"That's not true," said Cav.

"But it is."

"Not of you. Of everything."

"You're tired," said Dash. "You're worn out. You're old. That's what juving is for."

"I'm full, my friend. I couldn't possibly be any fuller. Not if I lived another life, or another ten. I don't need more than I have. I don't want more. More would only push out what I already possess, and cherish."

"I don't believe that," said Dash. "You don't believe that. You never have before."

"So what if it does?" said Gunjita. "So what? You'll find something new to cherish."

"I don't want to. Do you really not understand?" It seemed so simple, so elementary. He was puzzled and upset that they didn't get it.

Gunjita was pitiless. "No. I don't understand. You think you're being heroic. This isn't heroism, Cav. It's stubbornness. It's idealism. It's fluff. Romantic bluster. No one builds statues to romantics."

"I don't want a statue."

"You want something. What?"

Freedom, he thought. An end to the work of living.

And time. Time to prepare. Time to get into the right frame of mind. Find the right zone, and take up residence.

True observation was fearless. It was egoless. You had to give everything, expect nothing in return. His hope and his prayer: to be present, fully, for the experience.

"Aren't you even a little curious?"

"I'll be curious when I have to be," said Gunjita.

"Maybe I'll meet the giant oyster."

"You're a child."

"Don't do this," Dash pleaded.

"Honestly? That's an option. I might not. I won't know until I do it, will I? I could always back out."

Cause for cheer, one might think. Gunjita felt differently.

"Take all the time you want. Do what you have to. I won't be here. You've had enough of me? Well, guess what? The feeling's mutual."

She started to leave, then stopped, and came back. She took Dash by the arm. "You heard the man. He wants to be alone. Say good-bye. Let's go."

• • •

They departed the station the next day. Gunjita's eyes were dry. Dash embraced his dearest friend and begged him to change his mind, at least keep it open. Cav hugged him hard, then faced the love of his life.

They stared at each other, like two old warriors, neither of them knowing what to say or do. Cav had tears in his eyes. Gunjita regarded him stoically, until she couldn't stand it anymore. She reached out and took him in her arms. They held each other tight.

Then a miracle happened.

Time stopped, and the world disappeared. No past, no future, no uncertainty. Just that moment. Just them.

Invincible. Unassailable.

An island of bliss in a sea of amnesia.

• • •

Cav didn't accompany them to the dock. One good-bye was enough. He was drained.

He did, however, have the strength to watch their take-off. Every second of it. Eyes glued to the screen, as though his own life were at stake. As the shuttle ignited, then separated from the station, and all went well, he felt a wave of relief. Not long after that, he burst into tears.

He had a good, long, exhausting cry, then fell asleep. When he woke, every muscle hurt. He thought maybe he'd broken a rib. Apart from that, he felt better. Refreshed. Ready to move forward.

Mixed with this, a faint misgiving, a qualm, a question in his mind. Had he been wrong to throw Gunjita and Dash together? His wife and his best friend. If it was right, then why was he having second thoughts?

He was jealous. That was why. Not terribly, but a little went a long way.

Old men had no business being jealous.

But it gnawed at him, like a call to arms, a gauntlet that life had tossed in his path, and that needed to be dealt with before he could have any rest. As if it—life—would seize on anything, however petty, however small, to assert itself and not be extinguished.

He wondered how long jealousy would keep a man alive. Would depend on the jealousy. His was sharp, but fleeting. It lived only as long as his eye was turned resolutely inward. Once it turned outward, toward his loved ones and their well-being, their ongoing lives and unfolding futures, jealousy lost its grip on him. The cord was cut.

The HUBIES would come next.

He felt freer than he had in years.

–NINE–

Elvis Presley died of coronary arrhythmia.
    Is that what I am going to die of? I don't
think so. Of losing my temper perhaps.*

Cav had not been lax. If he knew anything, it was how to conduct an investigation. He'd done his homework.

At last count, there were, roughly, a million ways to die. Less, to take one's life. Still less, to dispose of the body afterward.

You could burn it, bury it, eat it, or let it be eaten—by worms, microbes, molecules. You could put it outside, aboveground, preferably somewhere humid and hot, and let it be eaten there—by beetles, ants, vultures, jackals, and the like, and the weather. You could freeze it, then transport it to one of Earth's remaining pockets of eternal

---

*   From *A Heaven of Words,* by Glenway Wescott.

ice and snow, and tuck it into bed there. You could embed it in plastic. Drop it into a lake of tar, or of toxic waste. Compress it to near nothingness. Blow it to smithereens with explosives.

On Earth there were options. On Gleem One, orders of magnitude fewer.

Cremation was impractical and risky. Burial was impossible. You could stow the body somewhere, but that would only leave the problem for someone to deal with later. There were no carnivores on board, save one, and that one couldn't very well eat his own body if he were already dead. Not to mention that eating a dead human, regardless of the circumstances, was gross.

You could suit up and send yourself into space, point toward Earth, ignite the thrusters, and become a meteor in someone else's sky. A reliable way to dispose of the body, and a quick way to die. Too quick—and too painful—for his purposes.

You could avoid this by aiming the thrusters in the opposite direction, fighting orbital decay, and become a new planetary body littering the sky, at least for a while. Cav hated litter, but felt backed into a corner. It didn't hurt that he'd been leaning toward ending his life this way from the start: half-knowingly before his arrival on station, then through the long hours of gazing into space, into his heart and mind, awe in ascendance, terror in decline. The idea had been steadily growing.

He felt a shiver of fear and excitement thinking about it now.

Death was a journey, composed of little deaths, little steps along the way. Sometimes the steps were close together, tightly packed, and death came rapidly. Sometimes they were spaced far apart, and it approached at a crawl. Suicide offered a choice of speeds. It was the ultimate in self-determination.

Cav figured six to eight hours start to finish. Most people choose a quicker exit, but he didn't want to rush. Didn't want to drag things out, either. Figured time would do its own thing anyway. A minute could last a year; an hour, a second. Six to eight hours seemed about right.

He ran through the steps in his mind. Space suit, jetpack, airlock, outer hatch. Nothing fancy. A simple defenestration. Stand at the brink, take the leap, ignite the burners, and embrace the unknown.

It wasn't complicated.

Nothing to clean up. No hole to dig. No ashes.

The only thing left to decide: premedicate or not?

He had pills, but didn't want to take them. Preferred to be awake and alert, alive to every sensation, every thought. He wanted to be fully in possession of himself in order to fully appreciate the experience. His sole concern: he might panic, and screw everything up.

Panic was a killer of the here-and-now. It was death to contemplative observation. It twisted reality, made it frightening and hideous.

He wasn't panic-prone, had only panicked once in his life, and that was after waking up from juving, a fairly common occurrence. He doubted it would be a problem, but also knew that panic didn't care about intentions, that it had a life of its own, came when it came, suddenly, out of nowhere, without invitation. The smallest thing could set it off, and this was hardly small.

He was bringing pills, just in case. Not to sleep, but to calm the nerves, if necessary. Composure, not unconsciousness. That was the plan.

His came in the form of capsules. Each capsule contained hundreds of tiny granules that looked like poppy seeds, but pink and white, the color of cotton candy. Colors favored by Gleem, which manufactured the medicine, and had named it, imaginatively, NOCKOUT, or NOK, as it was commonly called. Not to be confused with the beer of the same name, which had the same effect, if you drank a truckload. The name was a nod to days long past, when it meant glamour, bedazzlement, wow wow wow. Just the kind of double entendre PR and marketing departments fell out of their chairs for.

The word was stamped, along with the helpful icon

of a sleeping beauty, on a sleeping beauty bed, on the capsule's protective, gelatinous shell. It was a mid-list drug—reliable, no-nonsense, and a steady seller. He'd brought enough to put down a horse.

He planned to carry four, attached to his helmet within reach of his tongue and mouth, but separated, so that he could take as many or as few as necessary. He unscrewed the top of the bottle and shook out a handful.

A bad idea. A mass of capsules spilled out and immediately dispersed, like a genie freed from captivity. He grabbed at them, but it was like grabbing at a school of fish, and he merely managed to drive them farther away. He focused on one. His hand-eye coordination was not a thing of beauty, but he finally managed to pinch it between thumb and forefinger, and pushed it back in the bottle. Then he got a second one. Thinking, *this is ludicrous,* like moving a sandbox grain by grain.

What if it happened outside? They came loose in his helmet, then floated around in front of his face, a total distraction and annoyance, not to mention out of reach of his mouth?

A setback.

The upside: better to know now.

What could be done?

Go without them. That was one possibility. But it felt like giving in, and also risky. Besides, he liked puzzles, even now, at this late stage of the game.

It wasn't much of one, as it turned out. Capsules and pills were made to dissolve. Optimally, in a stomach. Less optimally, in plain water. But water worked, particularly if you heated it up.

He didn't have to eat his medicine, he could drink it.

He tried pulling a capsule apart, with the idea of dumping the contents directly into a beaker, where they'd dissolve much quicker without their protective coating. But the halves were sticky and hard to separate, especially for old, trembling hands, and grains were no more willing to be poured than the pills themselves, and in fact much less manageable. They dispersed in a particle cloud, then hung there, like a swarm of midges. He cautioned himself not to inhale.

Subsequently, he didn't try what he couldn't do, and instead used the whole capsules, and a closed system. Keeping busy kept him from looking too far ahead, and second-guessing himself.

It took an hour under low heat to dissolve them, then another for the solution to cool. While he was waiting, the comm came to life.

It was Laura Gleem. He recognized her voice, which preceded her image, and the perfectly modulated cadence of her speech. He assumed that, like her image, there was software involved.

She looked the same as always. Pert, attractive, businesslike. Abruptly, the screen went blank. Moments later, someone else took her place.

At least it looked like someone.

The person was sitting up, if "sitting" was the right word, in bed. She, if it was a she, was the color of ash and nearly hairless. What hair she did have was stringy and valentine pink, as though dyed by a morbid beautician. Her body was gnomish and deformed; she looked like a gnarl of wood. She was hunched forward, as though she had no choice. No fat or muscle. Drooping, loose skin. Strikingly, there were grapefruit-size lumps on her arms, legs, and torso.

The figure was draped in a formless gown. Didn't seem to care if it covered her or not. A network of tubes and wires were attached to her, and ran off-screen.

He kept his composure, even as his stomach churned. He wasn't entirely sure who or what he was seeing.

Laura Gleem's voice answered the who. "What do you think?"

His mind, uncharacteristically, was blank.

"That bad?"

"Is this you? For real?"

"In the flesh. Such as it is."

"You juved a third time."

"I survived," she said defiantly. "Give me credit for that."

"The lumps . . ."

"Tumors. As you'd expect." Her mouth didn't move when she spoke. "At present, under control."

"How are you communicating with me?"

"With difficulty."

"Deep brain?" He knew it had been tried. Still a few hurdles, last he'd heard.

"I wish." With an effort—and considerable discomfort—she arched her entire back, too frozen in the neck to independently lift her head, revealing a thumb-sized appliance crabbed to her larynx.

"A plug-in," he said.

"God bless 'em."

"It works well."

"Well enough. I'm due for an upgrade. And you, Doctor. How are you? You don't mind my saying, you look like you could use an upgrade yourself. Did I interrupt your beauty sleep?"

"I've been working."

"Glad to hear it. Work is better than sleep. Better than almost anything. You get old, you appreciate that."

"It's true."

"I assume your work includes our new object. What can you tell me? Is it worth getting excited about?"

A moment of truth. He decided to lie. "The asteroid's carbon. Nothing exciting in that. The object is metamorphic rock. A collision artifact."

"It's rock?"

"That's right."

"Is it valuable?"

"Possibly to a student of astrogeology. To you, no. It's worthless."

She didn't reply. She could have been thinking about deep-space mining, about capital outlay, financial risk, unloading her assets, writing them off, and so on and so forth. Alternatively, she could have been thinking about calling his bluff. In her current ravaged state, she had the world's most unreadable poker face.

He waited her out.

"I'm sorry to hear that," she said at length.

"Yes. I'm sorry, too. I was hoping for something different."

"Hope sustains us. It's our daily bread. The only bread I can eat." She half-grunted, half-groaned. "Have you ever seen anything like it?"

"Like what?"

"This," she said. "Me."

"You look . . ."

"Unusual?"

"Uncomfortable."

She barked. "Don't make me laugh. I look like crap. A crumpled-up bag of bones. Like I've been picked at by vultures, chewed up, spit out, then fed to a compacter."

"You're in pain."

"I'm a disaster. Leading naturally to the question of what happens next. How to remedy the situation. Juving is no longer an option. Having used my allotment and then some." She paused. "Thoughts?"

"You're asking my advice?"

"Your thoughts. You don't know me well enough to give advice."

"Fair enough. A question first: are you on life support?"

"To a large degree. Yes."

"Stop it. Get rid of all the wires and tubes. Including your feeding tube, assuming you have one."

"Why would I do that?"

"Take sips of water if you like. Get someone to help, if you can't do it yourself."

"I can't do anything myself. Except think. I'm a thinking machine. A rabble-rouser. A visionary. You want me to stop. You're telling me to die. Commit suicide."

"Die with dignity."

"That's the best you can come up with? And if I did? How long would it take?"

"Days. A week. Maybe two. Little by little, you'll fade."

"I'll fade."

"You'll drift off."

"I'll drift."

"Yes."

"Slowly."

"Yes."

"And gently. You forgot to mention gently. And peacefully."

"Yes. All that."

"Like a little cloud, warmed by the sun. I'll drift away, and slowly evaporate. I'll become one with the universe."

He didn't reply.

"Do you think I'm a child?"

"I know you're not a child."

"It sounds awful."

"You could take something. Go to sleep. Hurry things along."

"Sleeping pills."

"Your very own. You wouldn't have to pay for them."

"That's cute."

"You're afraid, aren't you?"

"Of taking pills?"

"Of dying."

She could barely move her head. He'd been talking to the side of her face for most of the conversation. But something came over her, and she wrenched herself sideways, until she was looking him straight in the eye.

"I'm afraid of nothing, Doctor. Nothing. If I die, I die.

But I don't want to die. I want to live."

"You've proven that," he said. "Three lifetimes' worth. Isn't three enough?"

"Not nearly enough. Four would not be enough. Ten *might* be enough. *Might* be. You'd have to ask me then. How old is the universe?"

"You want to live as long as that?"

"Shoot for the moon, then negotiate. I'd settle for a millennium."

"You're not greedy."

The barest hint of a smile on her dry, cracked lips. "A little greedy. Tell me about H82W8."

"You have our reports. Everything's there."

"I don't want everything. I want your summation. How does it look?"

"You should speak to Dr. Gharia. She's responsible for the bulk of the work."

"I plan to. But I'm speaking to you now. Is it promising?"

"Too early to say."

"But worth pursuing?"

"Depends what you mean by worth."

"You're being cagey, Doctor."

"I'm being honest."

"I'll take that as a yes. I've been told that Dr. Gharia has left the station. I won't ask why."

"It's no secret. The work is done. The study is complete."

"Did she take H82W8 with her?"

"Yes. Of course. It's not ours to keep. It's yours."

"Just so. I intend to use it."

"In what way?"

"On myself."

"Inadvisable, Ms. Gleem."

"Not here. There. Where you are. Gleem One. Where it works."

"We don't know that it works."

"Where it isn't lethal."

"We don't know that."

"We'll find out then, won't we? I'll need help. Obviously. I can't do anything without help. I can't eat. I can't speak. I can barely move. I'm a fully dependent creature, Doctor. Do you know how that feels? Do you know what that means? There's always someone nearby. A person. A robot. Some other kind of machine. Beeping, spewing, watching. I'm never alone. I'm surrounded. Fenced in. Encased."

"You need privacy."

"I need independence. Without it I feel . . ."

"Trapped?"

"Lost."

"I understand."

"Disrespected," she added sharply.

"Respect comes from within, Ms. Gleem."

"Oh please. Respect is earned, Doctor. On a daily basis. Speaking of which, I want you to do something with those things."

"What things?"

"You know what things. The Raggedy Anns. The abominations. I want them."

"*You?* Why? For what purpose?"

"They're mine. I own them."

"They're no use to you."

"I disagree. They're historic. They should be preserved. Somewhere they can be seen. Viewed. Appreciated."

"That's a terrible idea."

"A museum maybe."

He stared at her. "How about a trophy case? Or a zoo?"

"Those could work, too."

"They're not animals. They're not souvenirs. They don't exist for people's amusement. They're also not yours. They're nobody's. Ownership doesn't apply."

"On the contrary."

"They're public property."

"I'd say not. They're kept in vaults. Private vaults. They're traded on the dark web, and the black market. Highest bidder claims the rights of ownership."

"In that case, they're mine. I purchased them. Paid for them out of my own pocket. You can check your accounts."

"You signed a contract, Doctor. Read the fine print. From the time you set foot on the shuttle to the time you touch down, with plenty of room on either side, everything that passes through your hands is mine. All property: real, intellectual, unreal, whatever. All of it. This can't be a surprise. So just do whatever you have to in order to keep them alive. Further instructions to follow."

The screen went dead. Seconds later, it blinked back to life. A new image appeared, the Laura Gleem known to millions: brassy, high octane, irrepressible.

"Tell me something, Doctor. How do you feel about pink?"

He felt dizzy. "Pink?"

"All my doctors wear pink. I insist on it. Pink for my doctors, pink for my nurses, pink for all my staff. Pink pink pink."

"I'm not on your staff."

"But you could be. Easily. In a second. You wouldn't have to lift a finger. Wouldn't have to move an inch. Just stay where you are. Stay there, Doctor, and I'll come to you. I need someone I can trust. Someone who understands me. Meanwhile, enjoy your solitude. There's nothing like it, is there? And what better place? Just you and

Gleem One. No one else around. No one telling you what to do. No one hovering. Free as a bird. I envy you."

• • •

The call left him deeply disturbed, for reasons both obvious and not. He sat for a long time after it, wrestling with himself. At length he came to a decision, and rummaged in the lab for the necessary equipment. Once he had it assembled, he poured the now fully dissolved and cooled sleeping potion into a boiling flask, lit the flame underneath it, set the timer, then left.

He had not intended to leave a message or a note, but the call changed his mind. He wanted to set the record straight.

He began by identifying himself. He absolved all parties of responsibility. His decision to end his life was purely personal, he explained. It was not meant as a statement. That said, his conscience demanded that he speak out.

Juving came at a price. It had political, social, and economic consequences. It put a strain on the world's resources. It put a premium on long life at the expense of new life and new blood. It widened the gap between the haves and have-nots.

None of this was news. But it bore repeating. At some

point people were going to have to find a way to pack more life into less time. Be satisfied with a shorter life span. A century and a half, say. Two, max. A radical idea, but progress rode on radical hooves. Civilization would be nowhere without them.

He paused at this point. He'd said what he had to say, but the message seemed incomplete. More a sermon than a farewell. But sometimes sermons worked.

And farewells ... well, they were never less than awkward.

He saved the message, then returned to the lab, where the preparation was complete. A tincture-size amount of concentrated NOK remained in the flask. He decanted this into a bottle equipped with a spray head, then took it to the cargo bay.

The HUBIES seemed instantly alert to his presence. As he approached, their delicate nasal hoods retracted, their nostrils quivered, and their eyes swung like pendulums, then centered on him. The air felt charged. Even the Ooi, ever mute and mysterious, seemed to be holding its breath.

He administered his potion to the HUBIES. Sprayed each of their nostrils inside and out, until they were saturated. Repeated this, emptying the bottle, then moved a respectful distance away to wait.

It didn't take long. Their bodies were pint-sized. The

potion was concentrated. First their eyelids drifted shut, then their chests stopped moving, then their hearts stopped beating, then they were dead.

He said a prayer. Emotionally, he felt raw and nearly spent. He unfastened their harnesses, and one by one took them down. He cradled each in his arms, as he himself would not be, then tenderly tucked them into the bed they'd arrived in. Their womb was now their coffin. He closed and secured the lid, lifted the case, then headed to the door. Then paused.

He couldn't leave without a parting word for their inscrutable visitor. He wished it had seen fit to be less opaque. He laid his palm on it a final time, thanking it for what it had been, what it was. Then he turned, and HUBIES in hand, left the bay.

The space suit was next. Getting into it was a workout; the boots, next to impossible. His back and fingers fought him every step of the way. He had to stop to catch his breath. At one point he thought he was going to faint.

If living was a chore, preparing to die was worse.

He considered going without the boots, going without anything, leaving life as he had entered it, naked and exposed. This was the last time he'd be dressing, the last time doing that most human of acts, clothing himself. Death was a journey of farewells. Internally, a shutting down; externally, a series of separations. He was no fashionista, hardly cared what he wore, but he did like a good pair of socks, and on occasion, a nice warm sweater, and it grieved him to part forever with those.

The space suit was bulky. He felt mildly claustrophobic. Worse once he got the helmet on and locked in place. Started breathing fast; heart started racing. Chest felt tight, like it was caught in a vise. He couldn't seem to get any air, and began to panic.

He tore his helmet off, and immediately felt better. Waited out the attack, then tried again.

The second time was an improvement. Barely a whisper of distress. Instead, he felt a flutter of excitement as he entered the airlock. The call from Laura Gleem had sidetracked him, but now he was nearly there.

His plans had changed slightly. He wouldn't be alone. The HUBIES would be with him. Attaching their carrying case to his jetpack took time and also ingenuity. It was large and bulky, but eventually he got it strapped on and secure. A minor adjustment for him, though likely a real head-scratcher to anyone who happened to come across them in the future. Not that anyone would: a speck of a speck of a speck in infinite space. But if. If. What would they think?

A signal of some kind? A fugitive? A messenger? A traveling salesman, haplessly—fatally—thrown off course?

It made him smile to think of himself as a puzzle for

someone else to solve. Wished he could be there.

He closed and locked the inside hatch. The flutter of excitement persisted. So maybe not excitement, or not only. Ignoring it, he propelled himself to the outer door.

Through its porthole he could see a wedge of Earth, its far horizon limned with the sliver of approaching sunrise. The Milky Way was resplendent, not yet erased. He felt a fullness in his heart. Then, unexpectedly, a lurch, followed by a scary pause, then a pain unlike any he'd ever felt.

He grabbed his chest, broke into a drenching sweat. Couldn't seem to get his breath. His arms and legs felt leaden.

An alarm went off somewhere.

Thank goodness, he thought. Thank goodness for alarms and reminders. He'd been remiss. He was grateful for the warning to set things right.

Everything was happening fast. Memories, faces, and sensations flew by and blurred. One moment he seemed to have all the time in the world, the next not an instant to spare. The alarm continued, loud and insistent.

A warning? Maybe not. In fact, it seemed to be more of an announcement.

His heart was giving out.

He was dying. Could that possibly be right?

Dying on the way to kill himself? Dying on the

doorstep? Before he was ready? Before he could realize his plans? Caught with his pants down, fated to be frozen forever in the act, the purgatory, of almost there.

What a joke.

The universe was laughing at him. How trite. How perfect.

The universe was perfect. It was beautiful, beyond belief.

This life—and it wasn't done, not yet, not quite—was beautiful. He couldn't get enough. Loved it to death.

That was rich.

He loved life to death.

Love flew out of him in every direction. Love, attachment, desire, connection—the names meant nothing—flew out: to Earth, to the stars, to the emptiness between the stars, to the dark matter and the dust, the fourteen dimensions and the fifteen cosmos, to all that was living and all that was not. Love flew, faster than light. So fast that it came back around, and wasn't done. He knew it wasn't done, because the alarm didn't stop. Like a wake-up call, a catchy jingle that gets stuck in your head, a song from the symphony of life, vinyl version, with a scratched track that keeps popping back, it kept repeating, repeating, as if to prolong the suspense.

He was ready to die, but also ready to live. There was a

balance in all things, and death at the moment appeared to have the upper hand. He had made his peace with this, was prepared to embrace it, but he had a passing thought, quite possibly his last: was it too late to change his mind?

The thought, impossibly, gave way to action. Marshaling every bit of strength and will, he clawed his way back to the inside hatch, unlocked it, then collapsed into the bay. It was all he could manage. He had nothing left after that.

He hovered above the floor, more or less on a level with the Ooi, which was nestled on its rock. He stared at it. He, and he alone, had believed in it, and given it life. Who was he, he had to ask, to give life?

He wasn't God. He didn't believe in God. Or wishes on a star.

Yet there it was. An inert, unresponsive, implacable splotch now glowing like the rising sun, like a comet's coma. Radiating heat and light.

A miracle. Like life itself.

He didn't ask why or how. It was enough to be bathed by its healing energy. He felt it through his suit. It warmed his skin, but didn't penetrate farther, unable to drive away the deeper chill. There was so much of that. Too much. And it was spreading.

But the Ooi wasn't done. It ramped itself up, burning brighter, hotter. Red, orange, yellow. It fought the chill and the gathering darkness. Drove them back.

But not far, and not for long.

The alarm kept sounding. Louder now than ever.

Death was knocking at the door.

The Ooi seemed to shudder in response. Then it drew itself up, rose from the asteroid, and began to vibrate. Then hum. The hum was unrecognizable, unlike anything he'd ever heard. From its own symphony, or rather the expanded symphony, the infinite, universal one. Musica mysterium. Heavenly and euphoric. It drowned out the alarm.

Death retreated.

But not far, and not for long.

Eternal darkness was like a fog that might lift for a minute, an hour, a lifetime or two, but in the end would return to engulf all. A fog of oblivion. It sent its lacy tendrils toward him now. They carried the smell of death. An honest smell. Awful, but beguiling.

It filled his nostrils, then his mind.

Death was upon him.

The Ooi refused to yield. It hovered above the asteroid, and seemed to melt. Bubbles appeared on its surface, and as they burst, he smelled something new in the air. Sweet but not too sweet, rich but not too rich. Fresh and deeply satisfying. A smell to put iron in the blood and hair on the tongue. The smell of life, which overwhelmed the smell of death, and silenced the alarm.

But only for a little while.

Like a school bell, signaling the end of recess, it returned. Like a barking dog, it wouldn't stop.

He was growing weary of the sound. Weary to the bone. He longed for peace and quiet.

He looked to the Ooi for help, but it had nothing more for him, nothing more to give. It had done what it could. He thanked it with all his heart, and wished it well.

The wish was his final thought.

After that, there were only sensations. A roaring in his ears. A pungent, earthy scent. A spreading chill, and something opposing it, the embers of a fire, pale red and ghostly pink, growing ever fainter. He saw a ray of light, felt a spark, then was swallowed by darkness.

–TEN–

Comin' through today
You know what to do
Go for what you know
You can't pass it by
Bringin' it straight to you.*

Gunjita stood on the banks of the Ganges, near Rishikesh. It was early morning. A light breeze carried the smell of burning wood, bone, and flesh, from an up-stream ghat. A snapping turtle, grown thick-shelled on its diet of turtle food and supplemental calcium, was bask-ing on a nearby rock. Downstream was a small sandy beach. Across the river a steep, forested hill gave an inkling of the vast heights beyond it.

The smell stirred a memory. Gunjita had not been an

---

* From "Comin' Thru," by Chali 2na.

eater of flesh for many long years, not since coming of age, when she'd flexed the muscle of independence, commitment, and fierce belief. A hundred and fifty years a vegetarian. A century and a half grazing, crunching seeds, eating nuts and beans, sipping nectar.

The memory: her dashing, rose-scented father was roasting a goat on a spit. She must have been a girl. She could remember the smell, and the feeling in her mouth, the sudden, uncontrolled salivation, the thickness of her tongue, the aching in her throat. Roasted goat, crispy, savory, and rich. Two lifetimes ago, and she could still taste it.

Two lifetimes, and now she was looking at a third. She felt like a book that kept getting longer, with more chapters, more characters, more drama. The book meandered a bit, but overall stuck to a fairly predictable storyline. It was the book of Gunjita Gharia, thicker, weightier, heftier than ever, but after two lifetimes not much different than it was after one.

The world had changed; the woman only slightly. She hadn't wanted to change. She liked who she was. More of the same suited her.

This was true of many juvers. Others saw juving as a perfect time to try something new and different.

This did not always go as planned. Newness was one thing to wish for, another to accomplish. The habits of a lifetime, much less two, were not easily broken. Juving was no guarantee.

What it did guarantee: a month of turmoil, upheaval, and chaos, as the body rearranged itself. For most people, a distinctly unpleasant experience. It was a shock to the system, and every part of the system, notably consciousness, unconsciousness, subconsciousness, superconsciousness, and the two other consciousnesses, yet to be announced. She was glad she wouldn't be facing it again. She understood Cav's reluctance. But if she could overcome hers, why couldn't he overcome his? What was she missing?

He wasn't weak-willed. On the contrary.

Something shiny and bright had robbed him of the big picture.

There was a lesson in this, maybe even intended: the big picture wasn't the only picture. There were smaller ones. Small did not necessarily mean less valuable or fulfilling.

Parting advice from her ex.

Novelty wasn't for everyone, but if she wanted to give it a shot, she could start small. Make a modest change.

Goat, strictly speaking, wasn't new to her. But it was new enough. The prospect engaged and excited her. And why stop there? Humans were naturally omnivorous. Physically, it felt right. Morally, it would bridge the divide in her mind between sacrificing animals routinely in the name of progress and the greater good, and being opposed to their wholesale slaughter for food. Eating meat, if nothing else, would end the hypocrisy.

She could try chicken. Pork. Fish.

Cow meat? Even cow?

Maybe not cow.

She could see Cav raise his eyebrows at this. *Not cow? Explain that to me.* She could hear him questioning her logic. Not meanly. Never meanly, always in the spirit of clarity and understanding. She'd loved this about him. Maybe one day she'd love it again.

Right now she was furious.

She'd been back nearly a week. On returning, had immediately buried herself in work, where she felt most at home, but her mind wouldn't stay on task, it kept drifting. After three days she gave up, and booked a flight to Delhi, then a train to Haridwar, then onward to Rishikesh.

The train was fast, solar-powered, and efficient. A new experience for her—not the India of her childhood. Pilgrims crowded it as they always did, as they had buses before trains, and the broad, beaten-earth path before motor vehicles. Rishikesh, holy city since ancient times, magnet for seekers of truth and enlightenment, was a point of departure for her. A launching pad. She'd left it for a life of research and academia, a life of science, which asked the questions she was interested in, the ones that seemed most important. She was a pilgrim, too, no less passionate, devout, and disciplined than other seekers of wisdom, other servants of the truth.

In the early days she returned home regularly. Then irregularly. Then hardly ever. The last time she'd set eyes on the Ganges, save from the space station, where it looked like the Snake of a Thousand Tongues, was what? Twenty years ago? Forty?

The sight of Earth from the space station never ceased to amaze her. She couldn't get enough of her home planet. Cav, by contrast, couldn't get enough of outer space. He seemed already to have cut his ties with Earth, even before they lifted off. She should have known. There were signs, but she had discounted them.

She shouldn't have gone up. She'd been tricked. She hated him for not being honest with her. In their long life together, what other lies had he told?

A young woman, a villager by appearance, made her way to the small stretch of sand downriver. She was barefoot, with an anklet around one ankle and three dots on her chin. She faced the opposite shore, pressed her palms together in Anjali Mudra, and moments later, without prelude, was standing on her head.

Sirasana. The king of the asanas. Unorthodox to do it immediately, at the very beginning of a yoga session, without warming up.

She wore a saffron-colored sari, which didn't hide her long legs, or rounded bottom, or the sculpted arch of her lower back, or her toenails, which were painted violet. She held the pose seemingly without effort, steady, statuesque.

He'd dumped her, essentially. Not what he said, or believed, but what it was. For some half-baked vision of his, a story he insisted on telling himself, as if dying were a sign of integrity and courage. For that he'd shown her the door, like a guest who'd overstayed her welcome. The message was painfully clear: an eternity without you is better than another lifetime with.

She was glad to be rid of him.

The woman came out of her headstand and stood with her arms at her sides. Her face was flushed. Strands of hair had come loose from her braid, and clung to her high-boned cheeks.

She'd heard from Dash. Twice since returning. He was being unnecessarily kind and solicitous. It seemed genuine enough, but she couldn't help being suspicious.

She'd also heard from Laura Gleem, who wanted her to continue her H82W8 work, and offered a deal anyone would be a fool to refuse, save for the part of being locked into Gleem—and Gleem's agenda, whatever that happened to be at any given time—for the foreseeable future. She'd have a free hand, except when she didn't. Such was the life of a researcher. Was there a better one?

The breeze shifted, and Gunjita caught a whiff of cloves. It seemed to be coming from the direction of the beach, where the woman was in motion again.

She had bent at the waist, and now extended a leg behind her. She spread her arms to the sides, like wings, as though she were embracing the air, then swept them backward, taking her upturned foot in both hands, and arching her back like a bow, face and chest thrust upward. Natarajasana, Lord of the Dance. A combination of grace and power, she seemed about to launch herself. Or levitate.

Without breaking the pose, she tilted her head to the side to see who was watching. Gunjita felt like a Peeping Tom. She smiled, then found something else to look at.

Cav was a man of principle. She had to admit she respected him for this. He stood by his beliefs.

Starry-eyed when she met him, starry-eyed to the end. Tolerant. Curious. A lover of all things.

A singular human being. An admirable person.

She stole a glance at the woman. Had an urge to say something to her, compliment her, or simply thank her for the beautiful performance. Beauty had been absent from her life. The woman had opened her eyes. Thank her for that.

Her thoughts were interrupted by a call.

It was Dash. He'd just returned from a delicate bit of surgery on a rare albino walrus, whose club-sized baculum had somehow gotten tangled in a bed of kelp. He went on at some length, then continued without pause, as though afraid that if he didn't talk, there'd be no conversation.

He was staying outside of Reykjavik. It was raining, as it often did. He had an appointment the next day with a farmer near Vik, whose sheepdog couldn't walk in a straight line, and kept falling down. A growth in its ear, the man had been told by a local vet, who'd referred him. Another appointment the following week with the company that manufactured Pakkiflex, looking for an endorsement for their new line of undergarments.

And more. Mr. Chatterbox.

Eventually, he ran out of steam.

"And you? How are you?"

"I thought you'd never ask."

"I'm sorry."

"I'm kidding. I'm fine."

"Really?"

"Yes. Really."

"You should come to Iceland."

"Why is that?"

"Before the ice is gone, and we have to change its name."

"Is Ruby there?"

"Yes. Most definitely. In all her glory."

"How is she?"

"Alive. Cranky. Forgetful. Forgiving. You should visit."

"And make her crankier?"

"You won't."

"Why not? Is she no longer your mother?"

"She's old. She's frail. She doesn't have much left in the tank."

It would be hello, good-bye. Another separation. How many more could she take? She, in the prime of life. The bud of youth. The time for looking ahead, not behind.

Not to mention who this was. Not many could nurse a grudge like Ruby Kincaid. No one more loyal, loving, or quicker to judge. Then again, Gunjita had given her cause.

Amazingly, the woman had yet to move from her pose, except for one arm, which now stretched forward and upward, skyward, as though in exultation. She looked lighter than air, heroic, angelic.

"I'd like to see her. Let me think about it. I'll be in touch. Thanks for calling."

"Wait."

"I've got to go."

"About Cav."

She was afraid of this. "Not interested."

"You heard?"

"I don't want to hear. Please. I don't want to know."

"It's not what you think."

He flashed before her eyes, Cav did. True to himself. Undimmed.

"I'm sure it isn't."

"You won't believe it."

"Good-bye, Dash. Be well. Take care."

She ended the call. Moments later, the woman came out of her pose. She glanced at Gunjita, smiled, and beckoned her over.

She had coppery skin, thick black eyebrows, dancing eyes. She smelled of cloves and ginger. Her hands were calloused. She looked to be in her midtwenties, and everything about her said first time.

"Want to try?" she asked.

"Are you a cook?"

"I'm a baker. Why?"

"You smell spicy."

The woman laughed. "So? Yes?"

"Thanks, but I don't think so."

"You can do it."

"Unlikely."

"Just bend." Lightly, she pressed the small of Gunjita's back. "Now lift your leg. From here." She placed her hand on Gunjita's thigh, gently encouraging it upward. The touch was electric.

"Breathe," she said.

Gunjita had stopped. "Good advice."

"Lift your head. Imagine a state of weightlessness."

"I can do that."

"If you want to stretch your mind, first you stretch your body. The body leads, the mind follows."

"I thought it was the other way around."

"You mustn't argue. You must behave." Her voice was stern, except for the giggle at the end. "You're a student now. You're here to learn. Broaden your experience. Expand your awareness."

"Okay."

"Am I right?"

"Yes."

"Good."

Gunjita could only hold the pose for a few seconds. She didn't have her Earth legs yet.

"I've been in space." She felt mildly embarrassed.

The woman nodded, as if she understood perfectly. "Even better."

Acknowledgments

Thanks to Carter Scholz, Steve Crane, Pat Murphy, Dan Marcus, Angus McDonald, Mary Barsony, and Kumar Gadamasetti. Thanks also to my editor, Ann Vander-Meer, and the good folks at Tor.com.

About the Author

© Rodney Rucker

MICHAEL BLUMLEIN is the author of four novels and three story collections, including the award-winning *The Brains of Rats*. His latest collection, *All I Ever Dreamed*, containing three decades worth of fiction, "will delight readers who enjoy a wide range of genre fiction . . . and thinking deeply about social constructs and how they relate to science" (*Publishers Weekly*). His acclaimed essay, "Thoreau's Microscope," appears in the 2018 book of the same name from PM Press, as part of their celebrated Outspoken Author series.

He has twice been a finalist for the World Fantasy Award and twice for the Bram Stoker. His story "Fidelity:

A Primer" was short-listed for the Tiptree. His first story collection, *The Brains of Rats,* was awarded Best Collection by ReaderCon. His novel *X,Y* was chosen for inclusion in *Horror: Another 100 Best Books,* edited by Stephen Jones and Kim Newman.

He has written for both stage and film, including the award-winning independent film *Decodings* (included in the Biennial Exhibition of the Whitney Museum of American Art, and winner of the Special Jury Award of the SF International Film Festival). His novel *X, Y* was made into a feature-length movie. His story "California Burning" is currently in development in Hollywood for a movie.

Until his recent retirement, Dr. Blumlein taught and practiced medicine at the University of California in San Francisco.

You can find out more about him at michaelblumlein.com.

TOR·COM

Science fiction. Fantasy. The universe.

And related subjects.

*

More than just a publisher's website, *Tor.com* is a venue for **original fiction, comics,** and **discussion** of the entire field of SF and fantasy, in all media and from all sources. Visit our site today—and join the conversation yourself.